# CHOSEN

## A STREET KING'S OBSESSION

A Novel By

SUNNY GIOVANNI

www.royaltypublishinghouse.com



This is a work of fiction. Names, characters, businesses, places, events and incidents are either the products of the author's imagination or used in a fictitious manner. Any resemblance to actual persons, living or dead, or actual events is purely coincidental.

Contains explicit language & adult themes suitable for ages 16+

Remember….

You haven't read 'til you've read #Royalty

Check us out at
www.royaltypublishinghouse.com
Royalty drops #dopebooks

# Chapter 1

Some chick that he couldn't recall a name for had just taken her tongue out of Diego's mouth and all he could hear were his friends in the second and the first row of his Escalade, urging him to go inside of the gas station and grab blunts and drinks. The night was still young for the group at 2AM, so any and everything was possible. After slipping his hand underneath the young girl's skirt to get a feel of her wetness, he gathered that it'd be the best pussy he'd had in a minute, and exited the SUV to retrieve their supplies they'd need for the next few hours until dawn.

The phone in his pocket buzzed while he trolled the aisles of Chevron but he paid it no mind. Whoever it was wasn't important if they hadn't been inside his luxury SUV. The clerk rang up all of the junk he and his friend Angel snagged for when they'd have the munchies. And as usual, the total was over $100. He pulled out his wallet, took his bank card from it, then slid it across the counter and bantered back and forth with Angel about tag teaming the girl; he basically fingered before he racked up all of their goodies.

"Declined," the cashier said.

Prince Diego wasn't accustomed to that word. His head slowly turned to the Arab and his cedar colored eyes locked on to the poor man who only swiped the card. Diego's anger was very apparent by his peanut butter complexion glowing a shade of red. "Swipe it again," he ordered.

As instructed, the cashier swiped the card and received the same error message. To be sure, he rubbed the back of Diego's bank card on his jeans and swiped it again. "I'm sorry, but it's still declining."

Diego pulled two other cards out of his wallet and tossed them onto the counter. "Those better not decline or else you have a problem with your fucked up ass machine." He seethed. Finally, he pulled his phone from his pocket and checked his texts when getting ready to send one to his father. It didn't make any sense. He'd gone shopping earlier in the day, and his cards were working just fine.

What he found was his mother in a panic. She'd sent four messages that didn't sit too well with him.

*"My cards are declining! What the hell did you do?"*

*"A friend of mine had to pick up the tab for me, and it made me look like I was fucking poor!"*

*"I'm going to call Ramone. This doesn't make any sense."*

*"Can you pull out of your whore for the night and come to get your mom? I RAN OUT OF GAS AND CAN'T PAY FOR IT!"*

Angrily, he snatched his cards away from the cashier and stormed out of the store with Angel short on his heels. He ignored his friend's questions and yanked open the driver's side door to his SUV and pulled Chandler out of the front seat.

His short and stout body almost hit the ground until he caught his balance. "What the fuck is wrong with you?" Chandler screamed at Diego.

"All you hoes, get the fuck out!" Diego shouted to the girls in the SUV. "Make it quick! Don't you fuckin' suck your teeth at me, bitch! Get your shit and get out!" Without caring where they'd go or where they were, he adjusted himself in the seat and buckled his seatbelt. "One of y'all niggas get the Febreeze at the back and spray that shit. We gotta go and get my mama."

"Okay, but you still hadn't answered me," Angel said with a worried look on his face as he climbed into the front passenger seat. "What's going on?"

"My daddy is up to some shit, bruh." Diego put the car in gear and burned tires to get away from the gas station. "All my shit is declining and so is my mama's. She ain't even got no damn gas to get home from the club. Shit don't make sense."

"You think he cut y'all off?"

"Ain't no *think*. I *know* he did. I just don't know why."

—

Christina rose out of bed and crept into her mother's bedroom just about six feet away from her own, and peeked in. The apartment was dead silent, and she rolled her eyes. Her mother knew better than to sleep without her oxygen machine on. How many times had she warned her that it was a dangerous situation to lose your breath without knowing so in your sleep? Instead of waking her up and reprimanding her, she eased over to the large gray machine and took the nostril mask off of it, fit it onto her mother's nose and adjusted the strings behind her ears, then flipped the power switch before leaving.

Christina didn't know what she'd do without her darling mother. Regina was an older woman with a list of health problems ranging from congestive heart failure to asthma. After trying several times for a child, Regina's husband left. But when she begged him to stay because they'd succeeded, he didn't believe her. He thought it was a ploy to get him to stay in a marriage he wasn't invested in any longer. That in itself left Christina never to leave her mother's side. At a young age, she promised that her mother would never spend another day alone or without love. Sometimes neighbors hadn't known which one was the mother and which one was the daughter with how 19-year old Christina was constantly on 55-year old Regina's case about what she ate, how much strain she was putting herself through, or reminding her to take certain medications because they were good for her. To Christina, she was just a dedicated daughter who went as far as turning down scholarships to attend community college. Even though her mother was in a raging fit on the day she chose a college, Christina waved off the tantrum and reminded her that they had no one else and that she would do anything in her power to make sure they never had to reach out to anyone or grovel for handouts.

Three hours after checking in on Regina, Christina was in the kitchen in her pajama shorts and tank top, readying her mother's oatmeal for breakfast while crushing up her 6AM medication inside of it because she knew that Regina would want to push them away like she always had. Afterward, she groomed herself and left her twists hanging over her shoulder. A simple black t-shirt and dark blue jeans donned her body with black leather Skippers on her feet. She took her mother's food into the room and left it on the nightstand, hoping that today Regina wouldn't wise up and refuse to eat. She kissed her forehead and stroked her headscarf to wake her.

Regina's eyes fluttered open, and she searched the room until she finally looked up at her beautiful creation and mustered a smile. "Off to work or class?" she asked through a low and raspy voice.

"Both. It's Wednesday, mama," she quietly laughed. "I have work from seven to one and class from two to five. I'll be home by six to make dinner. Your snacks are already packed in containers in the fridge for today."

"Thank you, baby."

"See you later, Mama." After another kiss, she briskly traveled into the living room to grab her keys off of the coffee table and her bag off of the couch to head out for the day. It wasn't going to be easy to walk from the Boost Mobile store where she worked downtown to her school, but she was used to it by now. It was either that or wait an hour for a bus that would have her late to class, and she didn't need anything to get in the way of her means of taking care of her and her mother, or her future. At least on foot, it would take her 30-minutes to get to school, and it'd leave 25 minutes for her to relax before focusing on the lectures for 3 hours.

—

Diego and Markiesha pulled up to the apartment complex that Ramone considered his headquarters. Diego remembered them like the back of his hand. Before his parents divorced, he was so close to his father that Ramone would take his son to work with him and trust him outside with the other children. In fact, the housing projects were where he met Chandler and Angel. They'd long moved out of the area, but neither of them would forget those long and hot summers they shared when trying to convince young girls to lift their skirts or put their tiny soft hands into the boys' pants. A small smile stretched across Diego's face when he thought of it. The summer was soon approaching again, and all of the little girls who ran shy of him were all grown up, and he was more convincing than he was as a boy.

Markiesha noticed her son's smile from the corner of her eye and snarled at him. It wasn't that she hated her son, but he was supposed to be her personal trophy with his looks, his wit and the fact that he was Ramone's only son. She'd won her ex-husband over by having his son, and was ushered down to the hospital's chapel in a wheelchair while she was still coming down from the high that her anesthetics had given her. So many women had their hearts broken when the DNA proved to be the same as Ramone's, but unfortunately, her shining trophy couldn't make her keep her baller of a husband. She regretted the pain, the long labor, the sneaky and deceitful things that she had to do in order to lock Ramone down every time she looked at the boy, who could've been his father's younger brother by 24 years.

"What are you so damn happy about?" she sneered. "I don't see a reason to be happy, Diego. We're *broke*. We have nothing."

"*You* don't have anything. I separate my allowance," he snappishly replied. "I know how to live."

"Oh?" she questioned as she whirled around in her seat to take her oversized shades away from her face. Diego's skin crawled when looking at his own mother. She still looked as though she were the 17-year-old that had given birth to him, with her makeup properly done and her manicure as fresh as the day she'd gotten it a week ago. His mother was a gold digger, and it wasn't hard to notice it with the way she wore her tight fitting designers or her habit of acting as though she couldn't touch anything unless it was expensive. "How much money did you spend on your whores last night?" she asked with venom in her voice. "How much do you splurge on your boys when you call your barber over? And how much do you spend on liquor in a week?"

"Shouldn't I be asking you the same thing?"

"No. Because I'm grown and I do what the fuck I want to do."

"Same here. Get out of my car." He opened the door to his SUV and Markiesha grabbed his arm before he could slide out. With the way he pushed his back into his seat and eyed her, you'd think that she was an annoying fan who was trying to harm the prince of Mississippi territory.

"You go in here and talk to him because I will not go back to the slums. You hear me?"

He eyeballed her hand and said through closed teeth, "Don't touch me, Markiesha."

The two had an intense stare-down before they both exited the car and traveled down the sidewalk and rounded the corner to the stairs to get up to the third level where Ramone held a 4-bedroom apartment— where he counted his money and distributed his work. All Diego wanted to do was get away from his mother. She was damn near stepping on the back of his brand new sneakers with how close she kept to him as though someone was following them or wanted to snatch her up. Every man who saw them knew who she was behind her oversized shades and underneath her $4,000 ensemble. They wouldn't dare to touch the ex-wife of Ramone Caraway.

Diego knocked on the door and elbowed Markiesha for her to give him some space. He could literally feel her breathing on his bare arm and it was getting underneath his skin. Had she been one of his girls, she would've probably been pushed away. At least he still had some kind of respect for her in order to keep his hands to himself.

When the tattered door came open just a smidgen, the tall and Teflon colored man saw Diego's face from the other side and asked, "What you doin' here? And with her?"

Diego held up his pointer finger for his mother to keep her mouth shut before his father's goon shut the door in their faces and denied them access to his father. "I need to see him," he said. "He in?"

The dark skinned man eyed Markiesha and snarled. He knew her, and he knew that his boss didn't want to see the woman who almost tore apart his operation because she couldn't keep her legs closed. And in the divorce proceedings, she tried to take him for everything he had and was even bold enough to hint at the fact that he was a drug dealer. To this man, Markiesha was trouble. He'd have to have someone to snag a few blunts and to pop open the brown liquor during and after her visit just to keep his boss calm. Against his better judgment, he closed the door and went to tell his boss who was coming to see him.

Diego looked over at his mother and tightened his lips.

"What?" she innocently asked.

"Don't do nothing stupid when we go in here, you hear me?" he quietly demanded.

"Don't talk to me like I'm your ch—"

The door swung open and immediately Markiesha was hesitant about stepping inside. The strong smell of tobacco and liquor; amongst other things that she couldn't readily identify, told her that she didn't want any of it to stick to her designer threads. Diego, however, strolled inside of the apartment and went inside of the master's suite where his father was sitting on a table while watching women who were clad in bikinis cut and bagged his product. Ramone noticed his son from the doorway and signaled for the women to leave so that they could talk. He then slid off the table and brushed the legs of his dark blue denims with his ringed fingers.

"I see that the both of you noticed your sudden drought," he said nonchalantly as he pulled two chairs from underneath the table nearest him. He'd scooted one close to his son and sat in the other, leaving Markiesha to stand in her Prada heels. "Tell me that's why you came by and not because either of you had the notion to miss me."

"For one, you didn't even offer me a chair." Markiesha worked her neck at her husband and placed both of her hands on her hips. "How are we supposed to have a meeting if all parties are not seated and accounted for?"

"Everyone's accounted for."

"But not everyone is seated."

"That be true, but what do you need to sit for? This isn't a meeting. A meeting is what happens when people come together to share ideas collectively. That's not what's going on here."

"Then what *is* going on... *Ramone*?"

"If you shut up and let me speak to my heir, then I'm pretty sure you can get a good listen in."

Markiesha sucked in a breath and threw her hands up.

Ramone didn't care for her rolling her eyes, but what he did care for was the cigarette that he retrieved out of the box on the table behind him. It wasn't going to be easy to look at the product of him and his ex-wife to give him somewhat of bad news, so the nicotine might've helped some. "Here's the thing," he began while simultaneously blowing smoke. "You're twenty-two now, Diego. I was supposed to stop supporting you when you turned eighteen. But I didn't because you're my son. You've become a little too comfortable. I don't want you ending up like that beast who's standing behind you."

"Excuse me?" she shrieked.

"D, nothing in this world is for free. You have to work for it. You're old enough to take on part of my hustle just to get your feet wet. However, you have to earn that spot. Nobody on my squad was granted a position just because. They had to put in work for it."

"I'm fuckin' broke," he said sternly. "I have absolutely nothing, and you want me to do what for it? Man, fuck that."

"You do have a trust fund I set up for you when I found out that you were mine." Ramone leaned back in his seat and puffed from his cigarette then. Unlike his ex-wife, his son didn't have a gleam in his eye when hearing the mention of money.

"Well… what do I have to do to get it? I'm in that thang."

"You have to marry."

"*What*?" Diego and Markiesha screamed in unison.

"No, no, no, no, no… Ramone," Markiesha opposed. "Our son is a bachelor. He's enjoying his life. I don't see why you can't just fork up the dough and be done with it."

Ramone blew his smoke and flicked his thumb across his nose. This was one of the times that he regretted ever claiming her in the first place. He was stuck with her until the passing of their son, and he hated it. "I don't see why you can't just shut the fuck up and sit down somewhere, and let me and my son talk."

"Pop, this is stupid!" Diego yelled. "How am I supposed to marry someone I don't even know?"

"I'm sure you have a stable of women."

"Yea, but none I remember a name for."

"Then you can do a speed dating thing. Go on seven dates in seven days. I mean, you are a prince. There will be girls coming from all over Mississippi just to get a chance to say that they've gone out with you once. And at the end of it all, we can choose your bride-to-be."

"Man, naw—"

"Then will you give him his damn money?" Markiesha hissed.

"Yes, ma'am. And a piece of my hustle." Though he wasn't speaking to Diego, Ramone's light brown peepers were searching through his son's for an answer before he could even speak it aloud.

"You got a deal," Diego said and shook his father's hand to seal their business agreement. In the back of his mind, however, he thought that he could get one over on his dad by randomly snatching up seven girls to date and choose one out of a hat just to say that he'd marry her. All for the likes of money. What he hadn't counted on was that his father was not only teaching him a lesson in his own way, but he had already planned out the seven dates in seven days' event before he closed his family's bank accounts.

"What do you want from me to get my cash?" Markiesha asked.

Ramone stood with his son and told her, "I want you to go to hell and find a man who's worth a damn. Fuck out of my face. You gets nothing from me."

# Chapter 2

While Diego threw tantrums every day for two weeks over his father forcing him to sign a binding contract, another parent was busy being sneaky when trying to control the strings of their child's life. Regina waited until Christina had locked the door before she took her sweet time to get out of bed, shower, and dab perfumed oil that she hadn't used in a very long time on either side of her neck, and dressed herself. Because she was short-winded after struggling to put on her socks, she opted to brush— instead of comb— her hair and tuck her strands inside of a tattered wicker hat that she hadn't worn since Easter 12 years ago. Clad in a velvet-like long sleeve sweater in the middle of Spring, faded light blue cotton jeans and a pair of sneakers that were more than run over, she fixed a brooch over the heart of her sweater and applied her dark red lipstick. The frumpy woman debated on whether or not she should take her portable oxygen tank with her to forbidden territory and decided against it.

In the purse that she grabbed out of her closet was a flyer that she had taken off of the window in her kitchen, read carefully and folded it before placing it in an inside pocket. When she saw that Ramone was promoting an event for his son, the only thought that came to her mind was that it was something that would get her daughter out of the house for a day, to distract her from everything that she was seemingly tied down to. The qualifications had been carefully considered by Diego and filtered by his father. Regina figured that her daughter would win one of the seven dates that would be given out. On the flyer it read that every girl or woman who entered must have the application filled out and meet the specifications. They had to be standing at a height between 5'1" and 5'7", between the ages of 18 and 21, neatly groomed, classy, must maintain dignity in public, gorgeous smile and must be able to hold a career of her own. All applicants must leave a picture behind with their application for careful consideration. There was not a shadow of a doubt that Christina would nab a date, especially when Regina used her old Polaroid camera to snap a photo of her daughter when she made her laugh, just for the shot. Christina, oblivious to it all, hadn't asked any questions.

When Regina opened the back door of their small 2-bedroom apartment, the Spring heat warned her that she should go back and change out of her sweater. Instead of listening, she pressed on and marched down the walkway with a smile on her face. Her daughter was finally going to get a chance to live for a change. Her smile was almost depleted when she reached the bottom of the stairs of the unit some of the tenants dubbed "The Tower". She looked up to the last flight of stairs and gulped. Regina should've taken her portable oxygen tank with her because there was no way that her 230 pound, 5'2" frame was going to make it to the top without passing out. For the sake of Christina's livelihood, she trudged on and took her time with each and every step. What would've taken some about 2 or 3 minutes, it took Regina almost 15 to get to the top and to find the door that an addict had told her to look for.

She finally calmed her breathing, straightened her sweater and fondled her brooch to make sure that it was properly placed. Then she knocked on the door to have the dark skinned man open it. Only when he did, he opened it a little wider than the small space that he allowed just to get a better look at the elderly woman who stood before him. She didn't look like a customer to him, and she wasn't holding brochures in her hands. She couldn't have been a Jehovah's Witness.

"Can I help you, ma'am?" he politely asked. "Are you looking for someone?"

"Yes, actually," she huffed. "I'm looking for Ramone."

He turned his face to the side when trying to figure out what she could've wanted. She did look a little rundown, but in his 27 years of dealing, he'd never seen an addict like her. "I'm sorry. What's your business with him?"

"Actually..." Regina reached inside of her purse and fished out the flyer that she kept and handed it over to him. "I'm here because of this."

He took it and unfolded it, scanned the back for the application and found that she wasn't trying to enter herself into the registry. "I do apologize, ma'am, but the registry has ended." He then took a step outside of the door and leaned closer to her, pointing at the small print on the bottom of the application. "You see; it was supposed to be submitted by the twelfth. Today is the fourteenth."

Regina sucked in a breath to try and convince him just to take a look at the photo, but there was nothing to leave her lungs but a series of jagged coughs.

Feeling sorry for her and forgetting where he was at the time, he pulled the woman into the apartment and sat her in a tall-back chair near the front door, and scurried into the kitchen to get her a bottle of water from the refrigerator. When he'd come back, he shut the door and kneeled in front of her while twisting off the cap from the bottle. "Are you okay?" he asked as he handed it to her.

She nodded as much as she could and took her hat off before sipping from the bottle. The cold water was welcomed by her parched throat, but it hadn't stopped her from coughing.

Curious as to what was going on in the living room he called his lobby, Ramone ventured down the hallway to see who had taken a hit a little too hard. But when he was close enough to the salt and pepper haired dame, he could hear her wheezing. That alone let him know that she had asthma and that a bottle of Dasani wasn't going to help her. He kneeled on the other side of her in his pressed dark blue 501's and lifted her hands above her head. "Now slowly breathe," he coached her. "Focus on an item on the wall and breathe." Ramone gave his henchman a puzzled look that asked, *"Who is she?"*

"She came by with a flyer. The deadline has already been closed," he explained. "She wanted to enter her daughter, I guess."

"Go and put her information in the back and I'll look over it. She made a sacrifice like this so the girl must be worth looking at, at least."

Without any questions, the henchman went into the second bedroom in the hall so that he could put the application and photo on Ramone's desk.

"Miss, I'm sorry, but the deadline was two days ago," Ramone told Regina. "However, because I made the rules, I'll look over her qualifications. I can't make any promises to you, though, because I'm not the only person who'll be judging this competition that I made for my kid."

"I don't care," she managed to say before she coughed again. "As long as she gets out of the house for a day is all I care about. Even if the guy who answered the door takes her out for two hours is fine by me."

Ramone gave Regina a onceover and figured out a way to play the competition in his favor. "Listen, I'll have Black to walk you home, okay? I'll look over everything and I'll be reaching out to you very shortly."

"Thank you," she huffed.

The goliath of a man who was revealed as Black— such a fitting name— reached out his hand to Regina and she took it. Ramone gently grabbed the back of her elbow to help her out of her seat and watched the two slowly descend the stairs. When they reached the bottom, he tore away from the rail and scurried into his office to grab the Polaroid of Christina to look it over. Then he looked over at the application and roamed his eyes over all of her qualifications. He knew exactly how to get Christina into the running, even though he had already chosen the three girls that he was allowed to choose. He'd call and drop one of them over some kind of discrepancy. If Christina was as genuine and as kind as her mother, he wanted her with his son. And hopefully, there would be a connection between the two, especially considering the fact that he was nice enough to give Markiesha a vote.

---

Black waited for Regina to walk into the house before he turned away to leave. He and Regina shared a few chuckles as they slowly strolled through the courtyard. He left a smile on her face that had been wiped clean when she closed the back door and saw, in front of her, Christina on the couch.

"And where have you been?" Christina asked her mother with worry in her voice. "Why were out there in the heat? And with a sweater on, mama?"

"I just wanted to get out. Take a little walk. Maybe look a little good while doing so," Regina tried to reason.

"You didn't have your oxygen tank or your asthma pump with you! Anything could've happened to you while you were out there!"

"Stop speaking to me like I'm your child!"

"I'm *your* child! And as long as I'm breathing, you will be okay, and you won't pull a stunt like that again, Regina Jackson!"

"Why are you home?" Regina fanned her off and waddled into her bedroom to flop down on the edge of her bed.

Right behind her was her faithful daughter to pull back her covers and straighten them, and then fetch her nightgown so that she could make her mother comfortable. "You never mind why it is that I'm home so early. And if you must know, they canceled class today. I don't have either lecture to go to, and I really needed them."

Regina looked down at her daughter as she unstrapped the Velcro straps from the top of her shoe and took them off. It was when Christina flipped her braids over her shoulder that she saw again how beautiful her daughter was. "Chrissy, this ain't livin'," she mumbled.

"Don't start with me," Christina gritted while removing both of her mother's socks from the heels of her feet. She balled them both and stuck them into the toes of her mother's sneakers.

"You know what I mean. You wake up and take care of me. Then you go to work and school, and you come home and take care of me some more before you can get some shut eye. You have no friends, no—"

"You *are* my friend, mama," she said sternly as she rose from the floor. "When I wake up in the morning and take my first breath, I *am* living. Don't ever forget that."

"You're a beautiful young woman who needs to go out and experience life—"

"I am experiencing it!" she suddenly shouted. "I'm not leaving you behind like everybody else! I won't do it! So what, I don't have a life outside of these walls! You really think I want something to distract me from taking care of the only family I have? Forget about it! You only get one mother, mama! *One*! Don't do this to me!"

"I'm the anchor that keeps you here—"

"I'm not listening to this." Christina left the room after feeling like her mother wouldn't take her opinion into consideration. But she should've stopped to understand Regina's points before storming off.

"Chrissy, I didn't mean to upset you!" Regina bellowed. "I just don't want to be the reason that you don't have anything when I'm gone!"

"And where are you going?" Christina rounded the corner and leaned against the panel of the door with her head cocked to the side. "I don't think that you understand how valuable you are to me. I have my life all figured out, *Ms. Jackson*. I'll leave school within the next two years and give myself two more after that at a firm somewhere. But not until I hire someone to sit with you while I'm away. Then I'll open my own firm just afterward. When I'm thirty, you'll have your son-in-law and grandkids. Capeesh?"

"That's eleven years from now."

"I know. So you'll have to wait until then. For now, it's just me and you and dinner while watching Perry Mason tonight. The way that things were meant to be. And honestly, sometimes I like to tell myself that I'm glad your ex-husband left because he wouldn't know how to take care of you. You may see you as an anchor, but I see you as my mother. You may think that I'm squandering my life, but I see that I'm doing my God-given duty as a child by taking care of my mother at all cost. Don't back-talk the Master, mama." Christina winked and blew her mother a kiss before retreating to the kitchen to prepare an early dinner. If only she knew what was about to happen in her life a week from the day.

---

The day was almost hell for Christina when she walked into the house with her satchel hanging her waist, and with four grocery bags in each hand. Her cellphone rang inside her back pocket, and she rushed into the kitchen to drop the bags and answer for her caller. She thought that maybe it was her job accepting her request for Sunday off because it was her mother's birthday, but it had been a number she hadn't registered. She smoothed her braids to the back and tripped over the grocery bags on the floor when trying to figure out who had been calling her. "Hello?" she answered skeptically and leaned against the sink to listen.

"Christina Jackson?" the man on the other end asked.

"Yes? This is she."

"This is Ramone, The Duke, and I just wanted you to know that you have been selected amongst two-thousand girls and young women to go on a date with my son."

"What? Is this some kind of a joke?"

"Not at all. Please be ready on Thursday night by seven. Have a good night." Ramone hung up on her and left her standing there with a dropped jaw.

So many questions scattered her thoughts. She knew who Ramone, The Duke was. He was a man who sold drugs in the community but made sure that the people inside of her government owned apartment complex were fed. He even had a lunch program for the children during the Summer and after school just to make sure they were okay. Her most memorable moment was when he paid everyone who was over the age of 40's light bills one month. Christina had no idea that he had a son. Better yet, she hadn't known about any entry.

"Mama!" she screamed and leaped over the bags in the kitchen to get down the hall and into her mother's room.

Regina sat in bed with her covers up to her chest and crochet needles in her hands. She looked up at her daughter and smiled.

"What did you do?" she asked, quickly approaching the side of the bed.

"What do you mean?" Regina laughed. "I've been sitting here knitting and crocheting all day."

"You know what I mean. That's where you were the other day, wasn't it? You went to see Ramone about that dating flyer?"

Regina hadn't answered. She kept her smile intact, not wanting to get herself into trouble.

"I didn't know he had a son!" Christina panicked as she paced. "I thought the flyer was for him to find a new wife. Mama, why would you enter me?"

"Because you need to go out, baby."

"And who's going to look after you when I'm gone?"

"I can look after myself."

"Yea, right. You might as well call him yourself and tell him that I withdrew because of my work schedule. I can't go."

"That's too bad because I'm not doing that."

"If you don't, I will."

"And if you do, I'll move out and go to an assistant living facility."

"You wouldn't," she sneered.

Regina laid her needles and yarn on her lap and leaned forward. "Try me, Christina Jackson."

"Uuugh!" Christina stormed off to the kitchen and slapped the wall before she left.

Regina was quite content with her underhanded behavior. She leaned back and continued her latest masterpiece.

---

Angel knocked on his bedroom door while rubbing his goatee and leaned against the pane. Diego had been inside for almost an hour and his time was running out. "Pull out and let's go!" he laughed.

The young girl on her knees for Diego was only down there because there was a promise that he could get her into the contest to become his wife. Had she known that he was lying she would've turned away from him and wouldn't have gotten into his car in the first place. Unfortunately for Angel, all of the angry and deceived women would always come back to his home because Diego never allowed them inside of his house. Had any of them known where he lived his property would've been damaged time and time again.

After letting off a load within the girl's jaws, he situated his manhood inside his boxers and buckled his belt. "Somebody will take you home," he said before leaving the room. He didn't care for her. He hadn't even cared for the fourth date that he was about to have with some unknown girl who was most likely after his dick and his money. He just wanted to get it over with so that he could get his trust fund and a part of his father's hustle to keep him stable for the rest of his life.

Almost 30-minutes later, Angel let him out of the Escalade and escorted him inside. "You got your condoms for after, right?" he asked his best friend.

"You know I do," Diego laughed as he pushed the swivel doors to the eatery to enter.

"I'll be at the bar. Text me under the table if you need a quick exit. I'll have your excuse ready."

Diego stopped just shy of the host's podium and shook his head. "I feel like this shit is pointless," he expressed. "I don't see myself being with any of these hoes for at least five years just so that I'd say

I gave marriage a shot. My nigga, I'd kill myself before I let that happen. I have three more dates after this, and so far, I don't see myself lying with any of them."

A light flashed in front of Angel and he took his dark green orbs to the swivel door. Noticing the Decepticon emblem on the side of the GMC, he knew that it was Black with his friend's next girl. He slapped his hand down onto Diego's shoulder and nodded in the direction of the door behind him. "Looks like you don't have any more time to contemplate. She's here."

"Shit," Diego huffed, running his hand down his face. "What's her name again?"

Angel pulled his phone from his pocket and checked his Notes application. "Uuuh... her name is Christina. She's nineteen and she's a college student. Her hobbies include painting, sketching and photography."

"Boring than a motherfucker, man."

"She lives at home with her disabled mother."

"See, and this is the shit I'm talkin' about. If I was doing this shit for real, do you think that I would want to have somebody's mama shacked up with us, A?"

"Just take it easy," he chuckled. "At least she's thick and fine as fuck. Smash one good time and get it out of your system." Then Angel left his friend standing there at the door and took his place at the bar. Unlike other times, he chose a spot closest to the tables, at the end, so that he could get a good view of Christina when she walked in and even when they sat.

Christina herself came up with every excuse in the book before leaving the house as to why she couldn't go. It hadn't worked. Regina basically kicked her out of the house with the promise that she would text her every 30 minutes to let her child know that she was okay and that she was on track.

When Christina's eyes fell upon the 6'2" stallion known as Diego, the Dutch, her jaw hadn't fallen open and her mouth didn't water like all of the others. Her mind was on her mother, and her mother already fucked up the communication when she hadn't replied to Christina's message after Black pulled away from the curb.

"Diego," he introduced himself when she was close enough. He reached his hand out to her, and she took it.

"Christina," she replied with a weak smile.

"Are you ready to eat yet, or would you like to sit and talk at the bar?"

"I'm nineteen." She cocked a brow at him and took a step back. It was evident that he hadn't done his research on her, even though Angel had just told him everything that he needed to know about her in order to keep a conversation going.

"Right!" he lightly chuckled and pulled her along to a designated table where the lights were low and where no one would bother them but the waiter.

Christina pulled out her own chair. She hadn't been used to dating etiquette.

Diego screwed up his face at her and took his seat. He figured he could just fly through it all and be done with it. "So, tell me a little about yourself," he said and sipped from a champagne glass that was half-filled with water.

"Well, of course, you know that I'm nineteen now," she replied. "Uhh, I'm an amateur photographer and painter. I love art. Period. I take care of my mother, and I'm in college."

"Why do you love art?"

"Because it's an expression of life." She took her eyes from him and looked at her phone at the side of her. Her mother had finally replied to her message, but it was a series of letters and numbers. She squinted her eyes at it and frowned. Whatever Diego was saying wasn't important. She replied to her mother's message by asking her if she was okay and sent it. Then she sent a message to her neighbor so that she could go and check on Regina for her.

"Hello?" he said rudely. "Christina, I'm up here. Whatever's in your phone isn't that important. What are you doing, puttin' up a pic of our feet on Instagram?"

"What?"

"All I'm saying is that this is a date. I mean, you already came in here looking homely as fuck. The least you could do is try and hold a conversation if you want this spot."

The left corner of Christina's top lip rose and her eyes narrowed. "My mother is more important than you and whatever this is. And homely? Excuse me because I don't show my skin, but I'd rather dress in fitting jeans and a t-shirt over trying to look pretty for some pompous ass guy that I don't even know. Thank you for this so called date, but this is over."

"Come on, shawty. If you got a nigga, that's all you had to say. You could've been honest on your application."

"I didn't fill out a damn app in the first place. I choose my mama over all men. Including a nigga who's so full of himself that his daddy had to find girls for him to go on dates with."

"I get bitches."

"I bet you do, but none of them will ever be classy or honest enough. Why was I chosen? I don't fucking know, but enjoy the rest of your night by fucking off. I'm gone."

"Are you a lesbian?" he asked as she rose.

"Now I know you're crazy. Goodbye… whatever you said your name was." Christina briskly walked away from the table and swayed out of the swivel door to bang on the passenger window of the SUV.

Black took his face out of his phone to see the young woman in distress. He leaned over and opened the door so that she could get in. "Are you alright?" he asked her.

"I need to get home." Christina quickly buckled her seatbelt. "Please hurry. Something's not right. I knew that I shouldn't have left."

Black pursed his lips and waited for Diego.

"Why aren't we going?" she yelled at him.

"I have to wait for my boss' son," he explained. "He has to walk you to the door—"

"Man! Drive this damn rig and get me to my mama! Fuck him!"

Diego climbed in the back of the SUV and slammed the door. "Man, let's go. I need to get home. This bitch fucked up my night."

"Bitch?" she asked over her shoulder. "I'm going to let you have that, considering as how I don't ever have to see you again."

Black pulled away from the curb and sped to the housing projects to get the young woman home. After seeing Regina for himself, he knew how important her not being alone was. When he pulled into a parking space, Christina hopped out of the SUV and took off down the walkway to get to her back door. Diego caught up to her while she fumbled with her keys to get to the right one.

"Listen," he began.

"You see me going into the house, now leave," she said, and it was so fast that he wasn't sure if it was what she really told him. Finally retrieving the right key, she shoved it into the keyhole and opened the back door. She found Regina sprawled out on the kitchen floor and her lips were blue. She rushed to her and slid to her side on her knees. "Mama," she softly called her as she pat her cheek. "Mama, can you hear me?"

Diego stood there, regretting everything he'd said to her and every name he'd called her. She was the first honest girl he'd been out with. At that moment he was stuck in between punching himself in the face and trying to figure out a way to help her.

Christina's head rose from her mother's chest, and she screamed, "Call nine-one-one!"

He was stuck there watching the young woman perform CPR on her mother. He didn't know what to do.

"Call the fucking ambulance!" she screamed again.

He shuffled for a while until he'd finally located and pulled his cellphone from his pocket. He could barely get his words out when trying to give the operator the address and explain the situation. Still, he tried to calm himself when repeating and relaying information between Christina and the woman on the phone. After he'd hung up, he jogged to the front of the apartments to direct the paramedics to the apartment where the elderly woman lay there lifeless. Everything had happened so fast that he didn't know what his place would be. The last thing he saw was Christina climbing into the back of the rig with her mother on a stretcher, with tears cascading down her face.

# Chapter 3

Friday and Saturday's dates were useless. He ended up convincing both girls to have a threesome, and it only served as a tool to distract him from apologizing to Christina. It was apparent that all of the girls just wanted sex. They were easy and they had no insides. After each date his thoughts would go back to Christina. Sunday, however, had been filled with laughs and a little shopping after dinner. He liked Dena's style, her body, her smile and her laid back attitude. He knew that she was the one he could live his lie with, and if all else failed, he could at least be her friend. At the panel discussion on the following Tuesday, he made sure to stress his interest in her so that he could see where things went with them. Unfortunately, he ran into a brick wall at dinner between his parents.

"You need to choose a top two," Ramone informed him as he stuffed his mouth with shrimp. At least he hadn't given him another contract.

"That wasn't a part of the agreement," Markiesha hissed over the table.

"Pop, what the fuck?" Diego argued. "You never said anything about a top two."

Ramone, still feeding his face, dug into the satchel on the side of him and brought out a packet. He tossed it onto the table in front of his son's plate. "Obviously, you didn't read your contract," he said with a full mouth. "Page seven, section four. It's around that area. You choose a top two and spend a week with both of them separately. At the end of the second week, you and both girls will have dinner with me and Kiesha, and then we'll all sit on the following Tuesday to deliberate and shop for a promise ring. And don't fuckin' cuss at me again or else I'll rip your tongue out."

"You're going too far," Markiesha spoke up. "How dare you not mention any of this to our son?"

"Too far?" he chuckled. "How far is too far for money? I'm just trying to pair my boy with a good woman so that he doesn't end up with outside kids, STDs or gold digging ass hoes." He shot a glance at his ex-wife then. "With that comes a part of my dynasty and one-point-five million dollars."

"One point… five mil?"

Ramone pointed at her with his fork. "All *his*. Don't get it twisted." Then he pointed his fork at his son. "You already chose the Dena girl. Now you need one more."

After scanning the page, while his mother downed the last of her wine and rose her glass in the air for more, he looked up at his father. It didn't take him long to decide. Dena was a sure fire girl who would be easy to go along with whatever he had planned. Even if he squandered his chance just to apologize and give Christina a redo for her date since it ended tragically, it would be worth it to clear his conscience. Something he'd never done. "The Christina girl," he announced. "I choose her. Our date wasn't all that good because something happened to her mama. I want her."

Ramone stopped chewing and peered at his son with wide eyes. "Something happened with Ms. Jackson?"

"She collapsed or something. I just… I just feel bad for her, you know? I hadn't talked to her since, and I don't have her number."

"You just read the page, so you know that you have to call them personally and tell them that they made the top two, right?"

"Right."

"Then go for it. I'll give you her number. I'll check on Ms. Jackson myself. I need to go back to the office anyway."

"Pfffst! Office." Markiesha scoffed as she threw back her last glass of wine and fixed her fox fur around her shoulders. "If you call that an office then I live in a castle."

"Kiesha shut the fuck up—"

"I ain't doin this," Diego huffed and lifted himself out of his chair to head out. He'd rather go and get high with his friends before he sat to listen to his parents argue another day. Little did they know, he resented them both.

—

Soon after he left his parents, Diego was stretched out on the slope of a hill behind his condo with a blunt in his hand and his free hand behind his head. Angel sat on his left, Indian style, with Chandler on the other side.

"I don't see why you just don't tell 'em to both fuck off," Chandler stated with his attention on his phone.

"It ain't that simple," Angel opposed. "You think he wants to get out and work when all he has to do to get his money is calculating and snag a bitch to be a wife? I mean, it's a lot of pressure, but I'd take this over labor any day."

"But it comes with having to be a grown man and listen to mommy and daddy like you can't think for yourself. I'd break free and make my own money. Get a job. Go to college. Get a career. Be a straight-laced motherfucker for once."

"Shut the fuck up, Chandler. That's the pressure I'm talking about, but you didn't have to go into detail."

"It's all a game," Diego mumbled with a raspy voice as he released a cloud of smoke from his lips. "If my old man wants me to play this game then I will. It'll set me up, pay my college tuition, and then I can get a career and say fuck the hustle. I ain't like my mama. I don't want that nigga's money when I can get my own. Shit… I'm just enjoying the bitches for now." Just as he propped the tip of his blunt between his lips, his phone vibrated on the grass beside him and his father's alert sounded. He lazily reached over and checked the text message that had come through, and realized that his father had sent him Christina's number as promised.

Diego lifted his back from the grass and clicked on the number inside the message, pressed the phone to his ear and waited for her to answer.

"You've reached Christina Jackson," the voicemail blabbed. "I'm sorry I missed your call, but please leave a detailed message at the tone and I will make sure to get back to you as soon as I can. Have a blessed one."

Christina picked up her cellphone shortly after it stopped singing and saw that she had a voicemail. She rose from the couch in her mother's hospital room and held down her 1 key to see who could've been calling her so late and what it was they wanted.

"Christina, this is Diego…" She rolled her eyes and swiped her braids behind her ear. For some reason or another she finished listening to his message, as opposed to following her first mind to delete it as soon as she heard his name. "Ummm… I was calling because I had to choose only two young ladies to move on to the next round. I know that we didn't see eye to eye last time, and I said a lot of things that I really didn't mean… so I was just letting you know that if you're interested… I chose you to be one of the top two. Also, I was wondering how your mama was doing. Well, this is my number so please save it. Hope to hear from you soon. One."

She deleted his message and blocked his number. Afterward, she curled up on the couch and fluffed her pillow to travel back into Dream Land.

Diego periodically glanced at his phone, even when on the line with Dena to see if Christina called him back or sent him a text. Though he enjoyed Dena, he hadn't known what to think of Christina. How was she so immune to him? Even Dena had to complement him a few times before they sat and ate during their date. Dena couldn't stop lightly touching his hand and laughing at his corny jokes. It intrigued him. Christina, however, was hard, and it made him wonder why. She piqued his interest, and now she had him begging for a message or a call in his head.

—

Christina stepped off the bus, wrapped her braids around her ponytail and tucked the ends, then lifted the end of her black Boost Mobile t-shirt to stick it inside the underpart of her bra. The Summer was letting every person in the south know that it was right around the corner and that it wasn't going to be kind this year. She especially felt the 100-degree weather seeing as how she was wearing black slacks and sneakers as well, and her black and white satchel didn't help either. She'd had a very long day and she just wanted to get into the house to check her grades, eat and try to calm her nerves. After seeing her mother, going to work and missing one of her lectures, all there was left to do was kill over.

Christina stuck her key into the keyhole on the back door of her apartment and a shadow cast on the door from behind her. She turned and almost bumped into a light-skin young man with a caramel glow. His goatee and neatly trimmed mustache let her know that he was somewhat well-off, but she wondered why he held a large bouquet of roses within his massive hands that covered his baby blue and white Aeropostale t-shirt. She laid her eyes within his and fixed her mouth to ask a question, but he was already answering it before she could ask.

"Angel," he smiled, showing her a set of pearly whites that made her pull her earbuds out of her ears. She was so caught up in his handsome features and was dazzled with the roses that she forgot to take them out.

"I'm sorry?" she questioned confusingly with her eyes squinted and her brows pressed together.

"My name," he chuckled. "My name is Angel. These roses are for you, Christina. My boy Diego wanted you to have these. He was wondering why you hadn't returned a call or answered a text that he sent."

Christina fondly rolled her eyes as she had done when thinking of or hearing the name Diego. "Listen, tell him that I work too much to participate in any shenanigans that my mama got me into, so he might—"

"Actually, Ramone has taken care of that for you. Your job is safe and you'll be properly compensated for full-time hours."

"You have got to be shitting me," she mumbled as she dropped her head to squeeze her temple. "What the hell did my mama get me into?"

"Christina, this is a once in a lifetime opportunity. Diego is really searching for the one," he lied and had to stop to purse his lips before he continued to convince her to go along with her week of alone time with the young buck. "It's just that he sees something in you that he hadn't seen in all of the others. Ramone won't let him have his trust fund unless he decides between you and one other. Come on. Just to get it over with, why don't you?"

"Angel, was it?" she asked him, peering right into his handsome face so that he'd receive her message loud and clear. "My mama wanted me to do this so that I could go out and experience life. Whatever the fuck that meant. So you see, I can't at all be interested in pursuing anything with Diego. I came, I saw, I almost conquered. It's just the way it is." She pat his shoulder, but he wasn't letting her go that easily.

He gently grabbed her wrist and handed her the roses. An envelope hang from the back of the vase and Christina looked down at it. "Nondisclosure agreement," he said to her. "Just look over it all and call Ramone if you have anything you want to adjust or changed."

"You people don't quit, do you?"

"Not really. We're spoiled and entitled. What do you expect?" He winked at her and waited for her to take the vase and enter into her apartment. His insides cringed after she closed the back door. He knew that Diego didn't deserve a girl like Christina. From her bio alone on the application he read over, he wanted a chance to get at her. Her body was something he could squeeze and cherish, whereas he knew that Diego would just fuck her and leave her when all else was said and done.

He turned away from the back porch and pulled his phone from his pocket after being a good friend and phoned Diego. "Hopefully she'll take the bait," he said. "If you still don't get a call or text, it ain't my fault."

—

Christina had settled in for the night and turned off the vacuum cleaner in her mother's room before she could make sure that there was no laundry to do. On the way to the kitchen to put up her cleaning supplies, she saw the roses on the coffee table. She titled her head at them and adjusted the elastic band on her tennis shorts just to somehow keep herself away from opening the envelope she sat in front of the vase. Then she took her eyes to the clock above the TV in the living room. She realized that she had been home for 4 hours, and the only things she did was hurried and checked her grades, showered, studied, threw out food that her mother couldn't eat anymore, cleaned the toilets and vacuumed the entire house. She hadn't watched television or surfed the web. She hadn't gone outside to sit and speak to the neighbors. What Regina said had been true. Her daughter didn't have a life, and it struck Christina. Maybe she should live a little.

She'd gone over to the coffee table and grabbed the envelope and opened it. Inside was a packet of pages that she had to read and go over, so she took it to her room and opened her laptop to Google some of the words if need be. After careful consideration, she took her cellphone from the charger on her nightstand and leaned against her headboard to call Ramone. A week out of the house would have her paranoid, but if she could make an adjustment she only had two requests.

"Christina," he sang when he answered. "I'm guessing you've read your contract."

"I have," she sighed.

"You don't sound excited."

"To be frank, I don't see what's exciting about exploiting your own son with monetary attachments, but that's none of my business."

"Oh you've carefully read your contract," he chuckled.

"I have. There're only two things that I require."

"And what's that? You want more compensation for your work days?"

"No. I need a sitter for my mama, and it won't come out of my pay. The only way I'm leaving this house is if I know that a trained professional with a shining resume and at least ten years under their belt will be here. If not, then you'd have to drag me to hell and to the destination where I'll be meeting your kid. That's only if he wants me in the top two that badly."

"Christina, I'm Ramone, the Duke. There's nothing I can't do."

"Good. We'll start holding interviews on Monday morning at ten-thirty sharp."

"And your other request, Ms. Jackson?"

"That I am not to be bothered while going over my lectures. My education is very important to me and nothing… I do mean *nothing* will stand in the way of that. Not even your son. And also, I need my mother under contract to call me every thirty minutes or video call me so that I know she's okay."

"You got it, boss. Is there anything else that you require?"

"Yes, as a matter of fact I do. When all of this jive is over, I want to be left alone for good. He's not even to be within a thousand feet of me."

"And if you win?"

"Yea right," she laughed. "Your son is not the kind of guy that would choose a girl like me. I'm not easily impressed with what he has, and frankly he has nothing to offer me."

"Are you sure about that?"

"Very."

"Then why are you doing this?"

"I'm doing this because I almost lost my mama, sir. All she wanted me to do was go out and enjoy life and have a little fun. She didn't want to leave this earth and have me stuck here with nothing but the memories of work, school and the walls of this apartment."

Ramone carefully sorted through what she'd said. He'd use that too to his advantage later on in the competition. "I understand. I lost my mother years ago to the streets. You only get one. And when thinking of numbers, you told me that you had two requests. That was four. Think carefully before you speak. Especially when dealing with my son. All you have to do is be yourself and see who comes out on top. Hopefully you'll win."

"I don't think you understand anything I've—"

"Goodnight, Christina."

"Ramone—" He'd hung up on her, and she rolled her eyes at the wallpaper on her phone. "One of these damn days somebody's going to listen to me."

—

Diego had come off of the block and had gone into his father's apartment to turn in what he made in the heat. He had only one crumpled up $10 bill to lay onto Ramone's desk. Ramone picked it up and looked up at his sweaty prince while balling it up. When he swiveled around in his chair and threw it across the room as if he had a perfect jump-shot from the chair, Diego could've blown a gasket.

"You for real?" he squealed. "Do you know how long I've been out there in a hundred and two-degree heat for that shit?"

Quickly Ramone leaped out of his seat and grabbed his son's jaws with a firm grip. He said between clenched teeth, "You've been out there for thirteen hours and six damn minutes, boy. I gave you damn near a thousand dollars' worth of work, and you bring me ten fucking dollars? Most niggas get their fingers cut off for shit like that. Oh, you thought because you were my son that I was gonna let you slide? You had a quota, Diego. You were supposed to bring me two damn stacks, but you brought me ten funky ass dollars? My bitches make more money in five minutes than you did. How do you expect to get your own hustle if you don't start from the fuckin' bottom? Huh?" Ramone let his son's jaws loose and mushed his wet face with his wide hand. "You don't listen, you don't pay attention, and you're worse off than I thought you were. First, you want me to take care of you for the rest of your life, then you prove to me and everybody else that you're good with just fucking everything that walks without the repercussions. Now, you want me to take it easy on you and hand your oblivious ass a piece of something I worked my ass off for." Ramone banged on his chest and his left peck flexed through the fibers of his wife beater. "Your mi familia, Diego! You come from me, so I know you have it in you, but you're not showing me. Why do you think I trapped you with this competition? To make you work. Why do you think I bound you by contract? To make you work *and* think. Nah, you didn't catch on to that either. You might as well get the fuck out of here and start panhandling for change and marry a fucking no good bitch without any strength, skills and an ass that every other nigga done fucked. Go on and get out. And change your last name too."

As Diego's heart sank inside his rib cage, a scantily clad girl had come into the room and rounded the desk to remove his father's wife beater. He watched as she massaged his shoulders and stared intently at the Puerto Rican flag that covered the entire left chest muscle on his father's flesh. Ramone took everything to heart, and in that moment, his son realized that he had been wandering through life without anything to live or fight for. Maybe that's what Ramone was trying to get him to see. He turned away as the door opened again. Missing his face by an inch was the one girl who hadn't texted him. Seeing her mature figure and pretty face that was full of attitude made him feel lower than low after his father basically disowned him.

Ramone's head came down after he rolled it around his shoulders and stared at the bottom of the young girl's bosom. "Ms. Jackson!" he cheered when saw Christina in front of his desk.

She slammed a piece of paper down on his desk that contained one of the certified nurse's assistants resume. "I want her," she said sternly. Then she took the packet of paper out of her satchel and turned to a page that had been highlighted after Ramone adjusted it and initialed it. "Everything is signed and dated, and so far you've held up your end of the bargains. The only thing left is for me to hold on to mine. There's also an adjustment there that I think should be looked over and added inside the other contracts as well. If I hear the slightest pompous remark, I'm walking."

"Are you sure?" he asked her.

"Very sure. And in the event that I don't win..."

"You got it. He won't contact you or come near you inside of your thousand-foot radius."

"Thank you." She whirled around and eyed Diego. "You look like you need a shower." Then she closed the door to the room to go back to the hospital to be at her mother's side.

"By the way," Ramone said to his son. "Your electricity and water will be cut off two days from now. Looks like you'd better grind your ass off for it. You get nothing for free. At least one of your girls thoroughly read their contracts. Had you done that before you signed, you could have jewels, rent and free utilities... but you're oblivious as fuck like I said before. What are you going to do about it? Is this too much for you, Diego?" he mocked him. "You want to quit? If so, you can go and live with Chandler. But that's right... he lives with his mama. Well, then it looks like you can go and live with Angel. He's your best friend, right? Oh, but you can't. His mama pays his rent, and he can't have visitors after hours unless she approves. She still does popup visits, right? Then go and live with Markiesha. She'll welcome you with open arms. But you don't like her, do you? So then that leaves you to come home to me. You can't even do that because no one sleeps under my roof without earning their keep. That's why I live and sleep alone. You want to quit *now*?"

"I'll get your money," he said proudly when thinking of all of the closed doors he hadn't thought of before. "You can *believe* I'll get you your money."

"Sixty percent."

"What?" Diego scrunched his face then.

"My percentage just went up by twenty points. I want sixty since you want to half ass. Have it in by eleven fifty-nine on Friday night. Anything less than ten stacks will get your ring finger on my desk. I will make a man out of you if I have to drag your ass through mud and all."

Diego dropped his head and bit down on his bottom lip to control his anger. “Ain’t nothin’ in this life free, right?” he asked aloud. “I got to work for it, right?”

“That’s right.”

“So when this is all over with, I don’t want to hear sh… nothing. Because I’m gonna come out on top, regardless.”

Ramone leaned forward and took a wad of money out of his pocket. He pulled a $100 bill from out of the rubber band bound cash and grabbed his lighter from the corner of his desk. He held the bill at eye level and drew it into the flame from his lighter. His eyes went up to his son as Diego watched the $100 that he could’ve seriously used at the moment turn to ash. “Until you’re able to do this… you’re not doing a damn thing. Rise to the occasion or change your last name. I won’t ever shut the fuck up because you want to be a bitch about responsibility. I’m a father before I’m a money maker, so you better be glad that you have one, *boy*. Do what I tell you to and you’ll prevail. Until then… *you* don’t say shit. Get the fuck out of my building.”

Diego whipped around to the door and swung it open to leave. He had to come up with another strategy in order to get his dad off his back or else he was going to sink. He’d start by reading his contract.

# Chapter 4

Christina folded her mother's covers at her chest and stroked her silk headscarf. She didn't have the time or a brain cell to think of Diego and the petty little games that came with him. Her focus, like always, was on Regina.

"When do you leave?" Regina asked with a raspy voice.

"On Sunday night," Christina replied no higher than a whisper.

"Sound excited to be doing something else besides sticking by me."

"Mama, I'm already doing this competition bull... so please don't start with me about how much I love you."

"Well, today is Saturday. You should be home packing."

"Did you sign your contract?"

"I did, and I will promise to call you and keep tabs on you."

"I don't like how you switched up on me and made it every four hours."

"Even Ramone agrees with me that since I'm going to have a sitter and a caretaker that I shouldn't have to call as much. Heck, the nurse's aide is the one who has to text you every hour on the hour, not me."

Christina clenched her jaw at her mother, and a tall African man in a white lab coat strolled into the room before she could reprimand her.

He pushed his round frames up on the wide bridge of his nose and introduced himself to them both. "Good evening, ladies. I'm Dr. Morton. I am Ms. Jackson's cardiologist, and I have come to a decision concerning your need to go home."

"Good," Christina chimed. "Now tell her that she has to stay until she's better."

"Actually, she'll be with us for a while."

Both women stared at him with wide eyes. Even Christina hadn't expected him to say something like that.

"What's your definition of 'a while'?" she asked him skeptically.

"I've scheduled for Regina Jackson to have surgery on Thursday. We need to place a synthetic sponge in her heart for her ASD. It's when there is a hole in the septum between the heart's two upper chambers. It's called an atrial septal defect. I'm baffled that we hadn't caught on to it sooner, but I want to keep her for observation and make sure that everything is intact and stable before surgery."

"Are you trying to tell me that my mother is going to have open-heart surgery?"

"Not completely."

"Can you give us a minute alone, please?"

He politely nodded and threw a perfect smile at his patient before leaving.

"You're getting that surgery, and I don't want to hear another word about it, mama," Christina hurried and said as soon as Dr. Morton closed the door behind him.

"Here you go again," Regina complained. "Chrissy, you got to—"

"Be here with you."

"Stop hanging on to me!"

"Why won't you let me love you?"

"Why won't you live? Chrissy, I know you love me, baby, but now you need to go and live. Go on. You know I'll be okay. I'll be surrounded by professionals. Everything will be fine. Now go home and pack up for your week. Just be here before the surgery so that I know you're okay. You know I can't have my blood pressure raised. Please work with me. My anesthesia is wearing me down, so I can't hang on to an argument right now. Go on home and call me when you make it."

"This argument will commence six weeks after your surgery, Regina Jackson." She pecked her mother's forehead and picked up her satchel to leave. Tearing herself away from her mother's apron wasn't going to be an easy task, but she'd do anything for the only person she loved.

---

Diego regretted not seeing much of Dena before their week, with him working and sweating his life away. He had a newfound respect for every foot soldier on the payroll, seeing as how the majority of them had children to feed and clothe, and all he had to do was pay his own bills. At the end of the day, he only had enough money to stash and pay a single bill by the time he'd turned over what he'd earned to his father. He had to push harder.

When he'd arrived at his condo on Sunday night, he only had enough time to shower before there was a knock at his door. He pulled a white t-shirt over his head, brushed his wavy short cut hair and fingered his long sideburns to make sure that they were slick and sleek. He was still a pretty boy though he had been almost worked to death to stay afloat. Tonight would be his first night with Christina, and all he wanted to do was get his apology out and be done with it. Thanks to Angel, he'd be taking her to an art exhibit so that he could talk with her on her level, but in the back of his mind it was all going to make his mouth dry. He wasn't one for art or to discuss it. It bored him.

He brought the door open to see his best friend standing there with a smirk on his light caramel colored face. His 5'10" height was just beneath Diego's considering the height of his sneakers, but he pushed past him and entered the vast kitchen behind the front door.

"Why are we smiling?" Diego asked him as he closed the door and followed his friend with his eyes. "Did she cancel and it has you laughing at me?"

"Hell naw," he laughed. Angel lifted the cork out of a bourbon bottle and poured himself a glass. "She's downstairs in the SUV."

"Then what's funny? Why're you drinking? Angel, let's go. This art bullshit was your idea."

"You really don't understand what you're about to get yourself into, bruh." He sipped his brown liquor and lightly chuckled to himself. "This girl wouldn't let her mama sleep peacefully in the hospital because she was so concerned about her. And you really think that her or your daddy is about to let you apologize and skip out of the next six days of this week you're supposed to be spending with her?"

"That's the plan."

"This girl is focused on every-damn-thing. It's not like she's trying to win, but you need to ask yourself if you're ready to stop fucking with little girls and get with one who's actually going to be a woman."

"What the fuck are you talkin' about?" Diego complained. "We need to go. We're wasting time. I done been at work all damn day. I ain't got time for your cryptic ass messages right now."

"Fine." Angel tossed back the rest of his liquor and slammed his glass down onto the tray on the bar, then turned to his friend and popped the collar of his dark purple polo. "Let me say it loud and clear, D. You ain't smashing that one, you ain't playin' that one, and you're way in over your head this week. I'll be praying for you. She's about to fuck your head up. And your daddy was right. You're oblivious as fuck."

"I got it. I'm a dumbass. Can we go now? I gotta count up for my old man later on tonight. I can't do this right now."

Angel shook his head. At that moment, he hadn't known if his friend was really clueless or if it had all been an act. Either way, his sights were on Christina, and in the event that she turned Diego down, he'd be there to claim his prize. He'd never stabbed his own friend in the back or ever had the notion to, but Christina wasn't a girl for Diego and his bullshit. "This is all a game to you, and you don't seem to see how serious it really is," he mumbled before turning the knob.

"It's about as serious as your mama still paying your rent," Diego mentioned, right behind him to lock up his condo. "At least I'm earning my keep now."

"Don't you ever forget why it is that the bitch has to pay. All the bullshit that she put me and my sister through. She's obligated to take care of us now because of back child support. Nobody asked her to walk out on us when we were little and go off and make something of herself without letting the government know. Shit, we just let her make her little popups and shit to let her feel like she's in control. Don't act like I don't sell beats and shit. Who you think niggas come to when they want to record a mixtape or some shit? You ain't had to spend a dime on me unless you wanted to. I earn my own keep; it's just that a bitch owes me. It ain't the other way around."

"I don't think I like the venom in your voice for me." Diego followed him down the steps of his unit with the idea of tripping his friend being on his mind. “Where the fuck is all of this animosity coming from, nigga?”

“Get in the car and don’t worry about me. Put on your game face and do what you need to do so we can get this over with.”

Diego screwed up his face as Angel opened the back door for him. And when he slid in, he looked right into Christina’s worried face across from him. Unlike other Escalades, his second row of seats had been facing the third to give his ride a limo-type of effect. That way when his friends had the honor of driving his SUV, he could feel as though he’d been chauffeured.

Every word he planned on saying had gotten stuck somewhere between his lungs and his throat. He took his eyes from her round face and laid them on her ample breast through her V-neck designer shirt, that had a faded black vector of Tinkerbell on the front, as a force of habit. Then he’d removed them and put them on the white laces inside of his black leather Chuck Taylor’s and shut them. With the glow of her phone casting underneath her face, she made it hard for him not to notice that she was, in fact, a beautiful girl. He had to fight his manly routine of coming on to her inside the back of his SUV, because, in fact, had she been any other girl she would’ve been removing her denim shorts as soon as Angel had locked the doors.

“Hello,” she quietly greeted him sweetly.

It took him so much by surprise that he had to open his eyes and look over at her as if she had just spoken some kind of language other than English.

“I have those shoes.” Christina nodded at his Chuck’s that had a blue glow shining onto them from the stream of light that lined the creases of the cabin. Then she turned on her phone and shined the light over her feet to show him that she was wearing high tops. “Let me find out that you had someone to spy on me so that you could try and match my swag for the night. I wouldn’t put it past you, actually.”

“Uhhh… nah,” he stammered.

“Art gallery, huh?” She tried to change the subject when noticing that he had been knocked down a peg or two after their last encounter. “What made you choose that? You don’t seem like someone who is the least bit interested in talent.”

“Actually, it was my boy’s idea since you like art,” he answered.

"Oh. So you *can* speak English. You almost scared me for a moment. I thought that the bullshit you talked three weeks ago was taught to you and that you only spoke Spanish."

"What?" he quizzed; honestly confused at her sarcasm.

"You see, unlike you, I do my research," she explained. "Your dad's a Puerto Rican and your mama is a Black hot mess that nobody in my neighborhood is fond of. That was a racist joke to say that you only took after your father and learned Spanish and didn't speak English. I'm just trying to figure out why the cat has your tongue tonight. Care to share a little bit more of your English with me?"

"Has anybody ever told you that you're an insensitive asshole?"

"Are you sure you want to start this night off like this? I can have Angel pull over and leave you alone for the rest of the week, which would leave you in breach of your contract."

"You're just not going to make this easy for me, are you?"

"Not at all," she giggled. "But for real. Tell me. What's on your mind? Why're you so quiet now? I know you have a lot you want to say. If you didn't, you wouldn't have sent your boy to the Jungle just to give me roses."

Diego pushed his back into his fine leather and ran his hand down his handsome face. "I'm trying to figure out a way to tell you something, but I don't want to waste this opportunity on it. It needs to be special. So if you don't mind, can we start over and pretend that we like each other for the next few days?"

"Was that a 'please'? You really asked me?"

"Christina," he gritted.

"Fine," she laughed and crawled across the floor to sit next to him. Then she buckled her seatbelt and extended her right hand with a smile. "It's nice to meet you. I'm Christina Jackson."

Diego's lips stretched into an honest smile as he took her hand into his own. "Nice to meet you too, Christina. I'm Diego Caraway," he introduced himself. "It's kind of embarrassing to go on so many dates in such a short amount of time, but I have to make it work, you know? We're on our way to an art gallery that my friend up there chose for us to visit."

"Really? I just so happen to love art. Especially abstract pieces and street art."

"Good. Maybe you can show me some things because I don't like art at all. Honestly, it makes me drowsy."

"No way," she laughed. "It's the expression of emotions and life. I'll be sure to show you some things when we get there."

"Really, or are we still in character?"

"No character. I'm serious."

"Good, because I wasn't in character either. Swear I don't like art. I mean, comics are cool, but that's about it."

Christina leaned her head back and let out a cute laugh that Diego wasn't ready for. Neither was Christina. She hadn't shared a laugh with anyone else besides her mother, but Diego was so hollow and small-minded that it was a bit comical because of his bottom line honesty.

His eyes, of course, were on her bosom, and Angel peeped it in the reflection of the rearview mirror. He squeezed the wheel a little tighter to suppress the feeling of wanting to shout out how much Diego didn't deserve the beauty that sat next to him.

---

While Angel sat in the car, the night was going well for the pair who had originally been at each other's throats the last time they'd seen each other. Christina found out how dirty Diego's mind had been when he pointed at an oil painting of a woman and said aloud of how she should've gotten her third nipple removed before having someone to immortalize her. For most of the night, she had been laughing and smiling and bumping into him on purpose to make him stop speaking his mind when observing abstract work. She couldn't remember the last time she had laughed as hard or as much.

Diego glanced down at his pricey wristwatch and noticed, between the stones that separated the numbers on the panel, that they had already been there for close to 3 hours. The exhibit was getting ready to close, and it was nearing 10 PM. When he looked up, Christina was only a few feet away, hunched over in front of a graffiti piece with her braids tight in her fist to keep them out of her face. The label she was reading must've been that tiny and that long for her to be standing there as long as she had. He approached her and laid his hand on the small of her back to make her rise. "What's this?" he asked her.

Her eyes were on the word "REBEL", but it had smaller portraits inside each letter. Her stare was intense when pulling apart the piece with her eyes to understand the story and symbolism behind it. "It's by an artist named Geffie," she mumbled. "I love his work. I must have everything that he's ever done reblogged on my Tumblr page."

"You have a Tumblr?" He sounded surprised with his question.

Christina slowly turned her head to him and folded her arms. Her lips were crooked at his question.

He stared down, for the first time, into her eyes and was amazed at the beautiful swirls of brown and light gold in them. He realized that the only time he actually looked a female in the eyes is if she had pretty colors in them, but it wouldn't have been for long.

"You seriously have to start asking questions about me, dude," she said. "What? I don't look like I have a Tumblr? Or is that you have one, and you're all Tumblr famous to the point where you forget that regular people actually operate the accounts that follow you?"

"You and this mouth," he grumbled, taking his eyes back to the portrait on the wall.

"Your mouth or mine?"

"Christina." He laughed at her but kept his attention elsewhere. He was nervous to look at her again.

"You know, you're kind of handsome, Diego."

That statement made him turn his head to her and furrow his brows. "Kind of?" he asked, almost offended by the added on words she used.

"Don't get full of yourself," she giggled. "Take the compliment and keep it moving, Caraway."

"You ain't too bad yourself, Jackson."

"Why thank you."

Her smile beckoned him to lay a kiss on her chubby cheek, but he resisted thankfully.

The phone in his pocket vibrated, and he reached in to answer. "Christina, you might want to call your mama," he said. "You ain't looked at your phone since we've been here. I got to take a call real quick. I'll be right back."

Promptly she snatched her phone out of her back pocket and dialed her mother, cursing herself for getting so caught up that she hadn't thought to keep tabs on her. When Regina's voicemail picked up, it hadn't stopped her from trying to get through. She phoned the nurse's station and had them patch her through to Regina's room.

"What is it, Chrissy?" Regina grumbled. "I know it ain't nobody but you."

"You don't know that," she said jokingly. "How're you feeling?"

"I was okay two and a half hours ago when you called me. Okay, when you texted me. And believe me when I say that I'm okay now. I was just dozing off. How are you?"

"I don't know, honestly," Christina replied. "I thought that I would've had to choke him... but... dare I say that I'm enjoying his company?"

"Good. Now get off my phone and go get you some."

"Mama!" she hissed as she backed into a corridor near the graffiti work she had been staring at. "Don't use language like that."

"What? You're nineteen. You're grown. You've never had a boyfriend, and I'm pretty sure you don't want to die a virgin."

"Well, I'll have you know that I'm not a virgin, and I really don't want to talk about it right now. And besides, it was his idea to have me call in and check on you. I'm sorry for forgetting, mama. It won't happen again."

"It better happen again," Regina tiredly laughed. "I've been able to breathe since you've been gone. Don't ever apologize for living, baby."

"Yea, but I don't want to ever forget about you."

"You won't. I know you won't. And speaking of forgetting... your Uncle Buck is coming down from New York when I get home to see me."

Christina's frown turned into tight lips and her jaws flexed. She wanted nothing to do with her father's family. They'd made empty promises before, so this should've been no different. How dare one of them— her father's brother in particular— reach out after all of this time to offer up a lie just because of Regina's condition?

"Baby, are you there?"

"I don't want you talking to them," Christina whispered angrily. "Don't pick up the phone for them and don't reply to a text message."

"Baby—"

"That's the end of it. They've done enough. They weren't there when he left us with nothing. They were never there unless they were coughing up lie after lie or trying to give us false hope. I do enough to keep us stable, and I love you enough and take care of us enough for us not to need them or the motherfu... Mama, just please don't talk to those people." She had to calm herself; snatch her own leash before she ended up blowing up over the phone at the wrong person. "I didn't mean to lash out with misguided anger. Just get you some rest and leave those people alone."

"You're so overprotective, Chrissy," Regina giggled. "I love you, and I understand. If they come, they come. If they don't, I'm not worried about it. Now you go on and enjoy the rest of your night. I have to get some sleep. If it ain't you worrying me, it's them nurses in here every two hours bugging me."

"I love you too, mama."

"Goodnight, my love."

"Night." Christina hung up and clenched her phone in her palm. The Jackson family got under her skin and often she'd thought of sacrificing her monthly budget to change her and her mother's last names.

"You okay?" Diego asked her.

She was so lost inside her own hateful thoughts that she hadn't seen him round a bronze statue with a smile and approach her. She shut her eyes tight and opened them back as she nodded and put on a fake smile for him.

"You said that I should ask questions about you, right?" He surveyed her from head to toe and tipped her chin. "Well then... why you gotta be such a liar?"

"Excuse me?" She cocked a brow at him and took a sloppy step back.

Diego grabbed her hand and laced his fingers inside of hers as he pulled her out of the corridor and through the gallery. "You're so easy, Christina," he chuckled. "I know you're lying when you say that you're okay. Did somebody answer your mama's phone and piss on your screen or what?"

"No," she mumbled. "It's the other way around."

He pushed the front door open and led her out onto the street so that they could wait for an absent Angel, who had evidently gone joyriding. Then he turned to her and pulled her close by the back of her arms. "Tell me what happened," he demanded softly. "You were just fine, and we were doing so well until that phone call. What's up?"

She huffed and folded her arms over her chest. With it only being a week and having convinced herself that she wouldn't win and that Diego would stay away from her when it was over, she decided to open up to him. "What's your relationship with your mother like?"

"You want to know the real answer to that, or do you want me to lie to you?"

"The real answer." She playfully swatted at his chest and ignored how hard his peck was.

He pointed to one of the yellow diamond studs in his ear and said, "This one earring is worth eight stacks, okay?"

Christina nodded while trying to understand where he was going with his jewelry.

"My daddy cut her off financially, and her mortgage was due two weeks ago. Her mortgage is *four* stacks. It'd be nothing for me to take this earring out and sell it to a jeweler in order to help her. I'm wearing *both* earrings right now. Moral of the story, she's going homeless because my appearance is more important than her having a roof over her head. You get what I'm saying. You and your mama ain't like that, though. So tell me what happened?"

"That was... hellish... mean as fuck... That was evil, don't you think?"

"Not when you consider the fact that the woman didn't give a damn enough about me or my daddy to try and bankrupt him. The only attention, material or love that I'd ever gotten always came from my daddy. On Christmases, I'd hate to open gifts with both their names on it because I'd know that my daddy was lying. Markiesha Caraway didn't give a damn about me and then she proved it when she tore our family apart. Why care about a woman who would rather cry over being broke rather than her son's broken arm? I simply return what I get. And don't think you're off the hook. Tell me what's wrong."

She sighed and sat on a newspaper box on the edge of the street. It was only fair to give him a little of her backstory since he'd told his family business... even if that meant getting angry all over again when thinking of it. "Well, my mama and I are all we have," she explained. "She's the black sheep of her family because she chose to marry my dad, and his family is nothing but liars. My mama is having surgery later on in the week, and I guess my uncle decided to randomly call. When she told him of it, all of a sudden, he wants to bring his family down from New York to see her."

"And that has gotten you upset?"

"Just like you're angry at your mom for tearing your family apart, I'm pissed at them for closing the door in my mother's face because my dad fed them bullshit. She didn't do anything to anybody, Diego. All she was, was a good wife who was hoping to have a baby. That woman almost died bringing me into the world, and she was alone when doing so. Just one more complication would've left me an orphan. They didn't give a shit enough about her congestive heart failure just to check, throughout the years, to see if she was even alive. What's so different now? I just can't with those people."

"You let them under your skin that badly to where you had to mess up a potentially good night by lying to me?"

Her head whipped up to him.

"I'm pretty sure you'd agree with me when I say that I don't really care about most of the things that goes on in my life, but that's my key to survival. Sometimes you just have to stop giving a fuck. Look at it like this: You cared enough for your mama to save her life almost a month ago. They didn't. So don't worry about them. It's like you said, y'all are all y'all have. I'm sure your mama's a little offended that you forgot about all of the good that you've done and jumped out of character just to roar at motherfuckers who didn't matter."

Her jaw slid slightly open when she realized that he made sense. He wasn't quite as hollow as she thought he'd been.

His Escalade crept close to the curb, and he reached out to open the back door for her and waited for her to get in. The next stop was to the house for her until he'd gotten back. And after his phone call, he wasn't ready to leave her side just yet.

# Chapter 5

After sending a text to Christina to make sure she'd been settled inside of his condo, he patiently waited for his father in the office portion of the apartment. Ramone entered, and Diego rose from the corner of his desk.

"You're on time," Ramone chuckled. "Better yet, you're early as fuck. What's gotten into you? Christina told you to be responsible?"

"Can the jokes," Diego said forcefully. "I was having a damn good date on the first day until you called me. What you mean I was short a stack? Ain't no possible, damn way I was short at all. I kept my shit, I counted my shit, banded that shit and put it up. Even when I got here, I counted it in front of Black and had him recount it; then he weighed what I hadn't sold. I bypassed my quota by three bands when I raised the prices on them white boys who couldn't stop scratching their damn noses. I know for a fact I wasn't short."

Ramone sat behind his desk and clasped his fingers over the stomach of his red, black and white button down, and threw a smile on for his son. "I'm just fucking with you," he said.

Diego could've collapsed or rammed his fist into his father's face. Whichever came first. "You were... you were fuckin'..." Diego bit his tongue as hard as he could with his hand covering his mouth. "This was a game to you. You took me away from my date because you were playin'?"

"Yea," he shrugged. "I wanted to see how well you could handle yourself under pressure, and I also need you to help me with a new shipment right fast. We need to count this money and go over the books. You're gonna have to do this on your own in a little while, so you might as well get used to it. Every Sunday night."

Diego took in a deep breath to try and calm himself. He was tired of being pulled around on a string, and he hated the fact that he read the contract after he'd signed it. If only he would've manned up a long time ago, none of this would've been happening to him.

—

At 5 AM, Christina rose out of the bed in Diego's guest room and hadn't caught on to where she was until she placed her hand on the imitation crystal doorknob. She dropped her head and smiled in the dark. "Mama was right," she lowly said. "I don't have a life." Then she tread back to the comfortable bed she had gotten out of while lightly giggling to herself of how she had gone into autopilot once again, even though her mother was still in the hospital and she was at someone else's home.

By 7 AM, she couldn't stop tossing and turning. Breaking old habits would be hard, but she couldn't help it. She'd showered and parted her braids to twist the top of them into a bun and left the rest hanging down her back. Her attire of choice for the day had been a grey cotton crop top that hung off of one shoulder that had a dripping rainbow on the front of it, dark blue fitting denim shorts and white knee-high socks that had two bold red rings around the tops of them. She rummaged through Diego's kitchen to try and whip up breakfast, but she only found that he was the typical bachelor. There was no more in the fridge than bottled water, fruit, a champagne bottle, a package of lunchmeat that looked like it had expired long before she had even gone out with him the first time, and too many takeout and fast food containers to count.

Having enough of her struggling, she grabbed her satchel, slipped into her classic K-Swiss and snagged his keys from the bar that separated the kitchen and dining room. Then she jogged down the steps and used Google Maps on her phone to find the nearest grocery store. With only a 20-minute walk on foot, she brought back bacon, eggs, sausage, biscuits and pancake batter.

Diego's nostrils flared, and he stirred in bed when getting a whiff of the goods a few feet away from his room. His first thought was that it was a dream until he remembered coming into a lonely bed and having to check one of the two of his other empty rooms for Christina. He hopped out of bed, hoping that she wasn't burning down his kitchen when trying to cook, but to his surprise, it was the complete opposite. He stood at the corner of the counter with her back to him while he gazed up at the stack of 4 pancakes she cooked to golden perfection, bacon that had been nice and crisp, and sausage patties that didn't have a dark edge around them. While she shoveled scrambled eggs onto two different plates, he stared at her thick legs and thighs. She had more to offer than her body, but he hadn't known which made his mouth water more. If it was the photo ready breakfast or if it was the tone of this girl's build.

Christina gasped when she saw him from her peripheral and yanked out one of her earbuds, then laid the skillet and spatula she used inside the sink. "You can announce yourself, you know," she giggled. "How'd you sleep? When'd you get in?"

He shrugged and approached the two plates she had on the counter and ignored her eyes when they traveled down the ripples in the flesh of his abdomen, and grabbed her by the hand to pull her close.

She lightly gasped when her body mashed into his, and her eyes locked onto his. The two shared a stare while Diego wore a smirk all the while. "You're enjoying having me so close, huh?" she lowly asked him.

"Maybe." He winked at her and let her go.

She bit her bottom lip and rolled her eyes as he strolled over to the plates to steal a piece of bacon off of one. "You didn't answer my other two questions, Diego," she said.

"I slept good. I almost forgot that you were here until now. And did you know that you snore in your sleep?"

"I do not!"

"You do so. I peeped in on you last night, and you were snoring your ass off."

"Whatever." She fanned him off and took the plates off the counter so that she could take them to the table where they'd have a proper sit-down. "What's up for the day?"

"You have class in a few, and I have to get back down to the projects. We'll figure something out."

"Are you sure?"

"Yea. It's in our contracts that I'm not to bother you while you're studying."

"Look at you," she grinned. "Finally cracked that bad boy open, huh?"

"I did." Diego sat and scarfed down his two pieces of bacon, shoveled his eggs into his mouth and drizzled syrup over his pancakes. "That gallery last night," he mentioned. "Thinking of it made me want to find you on Tumblr."

"Did you?"

"Not at all," he laughed. "Text me your handle later. I'll follow you."

"I will. And don't eat too quickly. You're going to get nauseous."

"Tryna be my mama now. Do you miss yours or something?"

"Actually, I do. And I was thinking of going to see her later, but she probably would be upset with me if I did, over having fun and enjoying life."

"I think I can arrange something for later. I'll be back by the time you finish up with studying. Your mother left specific instructions in our contracts that state that you can't come near her unless it's an emergency."

"Sonofa*bitch*!"

"Looks like you missed something, Great and Powerful Christina." Diego folded his two pancakes and stuffed them into his mouth. "Gotta get out of here," he said with a full mouth as he rose from the seat. He then pecked her cheek purposely to leave syrup behind.

"Seriously?" she screeched. Even if she wanted to swat at him, he had already skipped down the hall and to his shower.

—

Diego dressed down today to fit the temperature of 102-degress. A black tank with a white Nike check broad in the middle of the chest, a pair of black basketball short and black and white trainers. He was tired; his body was sore, and all he wanted to do was sleep. His water bill was going to kill him with how many times he'd shower in a day now, due to the heat and how much he'd been working. With two other people being in the house within the next two weeks, he counted on having a fit when he opened the envelope from United Water of Jackson, Mississippi. In the event, he had to push harder. Lucky for him that the guys he sold to the night before called and left a voicemail on his prepaid phone and said that they wanted a larger order in code. He'd unload the two bricks; his father would give him in a few; off on them and get what he needed in order to cover his bills, stash money and still show Christina a good time.

After getting his two backpacks from the trap, he met his customers underneath an abandoned train track overpass so that no one could see him and that they'd have no proof that they were ever there. With almost $10,000 in his pocket, he felt that he could breeze through the rest of his Monday. Unfortunately, the dope game was like any other corporate business. His second phone was ringing off the hook, and he couldn't understand why.

He adjusted in his driver's seat and answered a call for a number he'd registered for a guy named Silk. The reason as to why he was calling was a complete mystery. "Yea," he answered.

"Slide through," Silk said. "I'm in the Oaks. I'll be waiting on you at the front." Then he hung up to leave Diego paranoid.

Just in case there was any friction, he had Angel meet him at the front of the apartments for whatever transpired. Silk had run out of weed and didn't want to go all the way to the trap for more, so he summoned Diego for his supply instead.

"Inflation," Silk laughed as he counted out $2,000 worth of bills. "I'm giving you three hundred more than what your stash is worth, but believe when I sell it, I'm gonna make this money back plus some."

"I've already caught on to that," Diego commented as he popped his trunk.

"Good. Shit, maybe you can make some extra dough by being a delivery boy. We ain't got that yet, and it beats the fuck out of what your daddy has you doing right now. Oh, and stay away from them white boys from Biloxi. Them niggas are sloppy, and they *will* get you caught up."

Diego tightened his jaw at the statement but was reluctant to cover his own tracks when dealing to them. All in all, Silk had a point when he had given him the idea of being a delivery boy. He just needed to sit and think about it.

After recounting what Silk had handed him, Diego had gotten into his car and followed Angel to a nearby eatery where he could finally relax from being on the move so much. It did beat him having to stand in one place out in the sun.

He sat in the booth at the diner and sipped on his orange soda while using the calculator on his phone. He had to make sure that his money would be right after turning in what he owed to his dad. So far he made $4,800 in profit, and he cursed himself. He'd have to make it work. Either he'd have to ask for more work or ask for a handout. After rent, he was down to only $1,500. He figured that he could stash $750 for bills and food, but that would leave him with the other half to spend on him and Christina throughout the week. He dropped his head and locked his screen when finally coming to the realization that he was going to have to change his way of living.

"What's up?" Angel asked him.

"Budgeting," he mumbled. "It's Monday and I'm already done with my work, but shit… with my old man taking sixty percent, I'm over here starving, basically. I got to make some cutbacks."

"You do. Especially before you get that high-class bitch Dena in your spot. I figure she'll want to go shopping at least three times next week. How're you gonna afford that?"

"Don't mock me," Diego gritted.

"Will it help if I paid the bill for our food? Because, you know, my mama pays my rent and all. That leaves me paying my own bills and buying my own food. If I don't hustle my music or rent out studio time, that leaves me with nothing."

Diego narrowed his eyes at Angel. "You're enjoying this, aren't you?"

"I'm just throwing out there that I've had to be responsible since before your daddy had to trap you within a contract for you to do so."

"So?"

"So?" Angel laughed. "You act like it's the end of the world when you can do other things to make your money. But who was the person who always told you not to get too comfortable? I think that was me. And why is it that you have a bank account of your own instead of what your daddy was giving you? Oh, that's because I told you to get one in case some bullshit happened. And don't you have money in that account, while you're over here trippin' out?"

"I do, but you know that's my Cabo money. We go every damn Summer. I'm not changing that."

"I think you should. Consider the fact that when regular people fall on hard times, they do have to sacrifice."

"What's your problem with me, A? You've been acting real fuckin' different lately, and I'm trying to figure out why you changed faces on me. I didn't hear none of this shit when you were gettin' bitches, eatin' and sippin' for free off my dime. But now that my old man pulled rank you're bein' a fuckin' dick about it all."

"I'm being a dick because you act like being on my level, finally, is fuckin' killing you. Like coming up off your throne is too much for you. You need to realize when you've offended somebody. Check yourself, nigga." Angel slid out of the booth and threw a crisp $50 bill down onto the table before he left.

Diego shook his head and left without giving a second thought to the fact that his friend had a blowup or basically paid for the food anyhow, to shame him. He didn't like how drastically life was changing around him but there was nothing that he could do about it.

—

Instead of asking for more work, Diego was told to be back at the trap the next morning by Black since Ramone was out of town. Black assured him that he'd let Ramone know that his son met his quota plus some yet again, and told Diego that he was amazed by how well he was adjusting. He dragged his tired body home and showered, then snagged a blunt from the drawer in his nightstand. Forgetting that Christina was even inside his condo, he'd gone out to the hill and sat to stare at the pond below and blow away the stress. Too much consumed his thoughts. Like Angel and his attitude, his dad basically raping his pockets and the fact that he still had five days to go with Christina before starting a whole other seven days with a diva that he was sure was going to spend more money than he had.

"It's pretty out here," Christina said from behind him as she strolled over in her knee high socks.

He glanced over his shoulder and took his eyes back to the sparkling waters. Then he pulled from his blunt and held in his smoke.

"I heard you when you came in, but I was in the middle of a paper. I was going to say something but—"

"You're good," he interrupted her, slowly releasing the smoke from his lungs.

Christina cocked her head to the side and took a seat beside him. She hugged her knees and fondly leaned her head over onto his shoulder.

It almost made him choke on the smoke he'd hurried and gathered into his lungs until he looked over and realized that she had taken her braids down. She'd picked out her crinkly locks and tied a bandana around the edge of her head with a hair band. It only made him wonder why women wore weave when they already had a head full of long and thick locks of their own.

"Life is hard," she mumbled. She took in the beauty of the pond and the little gathering of ducks that had been around, battling it out for a piece of soggy bread that Diego had thrown down there before he lit his blunt. "I have so much on my mind that it's ridiculous. It's difficult for me to stay away from my mama and I guess that's another reason that I avoid having a life in the first place. It's because if I have something to live for… then everything would make perfectly good sense."

"Did you just have an epiphany?" he sarcastically asked her.

"Shut up," she giggled. "I was thinking of it while doing my paper. I guess if it was just me then I would wander through life. That's why I don't fault you for being so spoiled, you know? You've had mama and daddy there with you, and I hadn't. Your dad has taken care of you since forever so this is a big transition for you. But let me tell you, life will always kick you in the balls. Hell, you've been stable all of your life and it's kicking you in your baby-maker right now, so I don't expect it to be any easier for me when all of this is over."

"How do you do it, Christina? How do you do what you do in a day without saying fuck it?"

"How do you know what it is that I do in a day?"

"You have to go to work and school and take care of your mama. It was in your bio on your app. I read it, remember? I don't see how you do it."

"My mama's my motivation," she replied as she swiped a piece of her hair behind her ear. "Just to make sure that she never has to worry another day in her life, I'm willing to sacrifice my own. It works out."

"Don't laugh at me but I'm new to this shit. I budgeted for the first time today, and I wanted to fuckin' hurt a nigga. I'd never been on a fuckin' budget."

"Life changes, you know. It doesn't mean that you're going to stay at that specific amount of money, but it means that you have to adjust your living to it for now. Just go harder and reach for more. That's what I do. And be lucky that it's just you that you have to take care of and not a whole other human being. You're still fortunate in many ways. Don't look at the negative, look at the positive."

"So if I chose you, would you be willing to live off of seven hundred and fifty dollars a week?"

"HA!" Christina laughed. "Boy, I live off of a quarter less than that in a month. Oh, Prince Diego. You have much to learn about this fucked up ass ball we call life. You got to be flexible. And you sitting out here wading in your tears and shooting yourself off to Mars with that weed in your hand ain't gonna get you nowhere." She pecked his cheek and lifted herself from the grass to go back into the condo. "By the way, dinner's on."

"Where're you gettin' the money to put food in my house?" he asked over his shoulder.

"See, responsible adults have savings accounts. I don't— nor will I ever— need your money. I have my own."

"Well, let me pay you back for it. Where are the receipts?"

"Fuck your money." She mushed the back of his head and jogged up the steps to the condo.

Diego was right behind her though his weed slowed him down a bit.

"Okay, I quit," she surrendered and grabbed the spatula to turn over the chicken she'd been frying inside of a large pot on the stove.

"Fuck my money?" he asked her as he made his way into his room to put out his blunt and lay it in an ashtray. He'd come back and wrapped his arms around her waist. Maybe it was his high that made him so bold, but he was lucky that Christina didn't push him away and oppose. "I asked you a question. You said fuck my money, Chrissy?"

"You're just so comfortable calling me Chrissy, aren't you?"

"Maybe. Now, answer my question."

She laid the spatula down on a napkin she folded on the countertop and twisted around to him. Her arms slowly curved around his neck and her face leaned into his. Her lips were dangerously close to his when she stopped and looked at him through bedroom eyes. "Sweetie… listen to me and listen to me well, okay?"

"Mmhhmm," he hummed, praying that she'd just lean a little closer.

"I work for myself and for my mama, understand? And even in the strangest occurrence that you just so happen to choose me, you'd better know that I have no desire of touching what is yours. Not now or ever will anybody stop me from getting my own duckettes."

"Is that so?"

"That is correct, sir."

He pecked her lips, and she mushed his face and continued to turn over the chicken so that it wouldn't burn. "You know you liked it."

"Let me find out that you have a thing for me," she giggled.

"I don't need to say what's evident."

"Can we sit out at the pond tonight?" She changed the subject entirely.

"Yea, if that's what you want to do."

"Hell yea. After dinner, maybe we can take our desert out there and just talk."

"Cool. I'll be looking forward to it, with your mean ass." He gave her a playful slap on the backside and skipped out of the kitchen before she could hit him back.

She started to swing, but he was a little too quick for her. She retracted her hand and placed it on her hip while trying to stifle her smile. She couldn't lie to herself. She was sort of into him too.

---

Almost two hours later— after the pair had spent the majority of their evening cracking jokes on one another, which made them slowly take down Christina's golden fried chicken, mashed potatoes, corn on the cob, spinach and cornbread— they were sitting on the hill staring at the lights from the buildings and houses downtown dance across the waters below. Each of them had a slice of cheesecake on saucers, and all you could hear were the sounds of their forks clinking against the china.

Diego had long made himself comfortable in a black wife beater and black and red basketball shorts, and Christina pulled on her dark grey muscle shirt and slipped into her black tennis shorts. The both of them had only long black socks donning their feet.

"My mama would have a fit if she knew that I was out here like this." She quietly laughed to herself.

"What you mean?" Diego replied with a full mouth.

"Look at me. My mama is old school. She's fifty-five. If you're underdressed, they all think that you're gonna get sick. Especially if you're not wearing any shoes."

"Then I guess we'd both get a good talkin' to if she decided to do a popup visit."

"Shit!" she gasped. Her eyes had gone wide, and she laid her saucer down beside her.

"What is it?"

"I left my damn phone upstairs."

"Relax," he chuckled. "I'm sure she's okay. My phone's in my pocket. If anything happened and they can't get ahold of you, the CNA's going to call me. You're covered."

"Thank God." She blew a hard stream of breath out of her mouth and brought her saucer up to have another bite of her store-bought dessert.

"I wish I had a relationship like that with my mama… but honestly…" He stopped stuffing his face then and stared out at that dark pond blankly. "I highly believe I wouldn't piss on her if she was on fire."

To Christina, that was a very hard statement to say about a woman who had given him life. Because it was too soon to pry, she opted to take his mind off of it to keep the good vibe she'd been feeling flowing. She liked more of the playful side of him than the uptight, mean and arrogant version of him. "Well... I hope you *wouldn't* pee on her. That's just nasty."

"You're so corny, yo'," he laughed, and bit down on his bottom lip when looking over at her.

She had her head bowed as she shoveled around what little graham cracker crust and cream cheese filling that she had left to eat.

He'd noticed her cleavage and his nostrils flexed. He'd have to fight himself again to keep his hormones at bay. Christina was doing something to him, and even though it was in his nature to take down his women on the first night, he fought to keep that part away from her. He'd never restrained himself. "You're beautiful, Chrissy," he said aloud before he knew he had.

She looked over at him with a small smile on her face.

"You got a big ass head, though, but you're beautiful."

"Oh, really?" she giggled. "We're gonna talk about heads now?"

"Yup. Goodyear Blimp-head-ass girl."

"You know what? I'm gonna let you make it because I know I have a big head. That's why God blessed me with a lot of hair. It takes the focus off my head and gives everybody something else to look at."

Suddenly he couldn't control himself anymore. He grabbed a fistful of her hair and pulled her head slightly back. His lips slammed onto hers, and he held them there for what seemed like forever. When he drew back, he expected to be reprimanded for his disrespect.

Instead, Christina sat her saucer beside her, pulled her crinkly locks behind her head and twisted them into a small knot. "That's all you got?" she asked him. "You can't do no better than that?"

"Word?" He was astonished with a cocked brow to complement it. He thought that she would've gotten up and walked away at the least, or slapped him.

"Word. Come here. Try a little harder than that. Your lips were quivering. I wouldn't have expected that from you."

"I wouldn't have expected this from you either, but—"

Christina hushed him by forcing her lips on top of his and making him so comfortable with a few kisses as to slide her tongue inside his mouth. She straddled him and brought his hands to the small of her back. He had gotten so lost in the kiss that he hadn't felt the erection that was growing inside of his shorts. When it poked her between the legs, she broke the kiss and slid off of him.

"Damn, Chrissy," he huffed and tried to readjust himself in his briefs. "What came over you?"

"The fact that you keep being gentle with me," she said honestly. "I know that a guy like you can't just take it easy with all of your women."

"Are you callin' me a hoe?"

"Yes. And I'm saying that you're not being yourself around me. Show me you."

"You should be lucky that I'm not being me. If I was being me, then I would've had you bent over the bar at Angel's place on the first date. It's just something about you that won't let me take control of you like I do with them."

"Is it because I'm mean, as you say?"

"That could be it," he chuckled. His phone vibrated in his pocket, and he reached in to answer it even though he didn't want to. When he saw that it was Dena, he rejected the call and sent it to voicemail. "How about we go up to the house now. My ass hurts and I'm full as hell right now."

"Yea, and Perry Mason is on."

"Who?" He screwed up his face at her. "Who the fuck is Perry Mason?"

Christina's brow rose. "You really don't know who Perry Mason is?"

"What is he, a VJ? A Vlogger? Prankster?"

She grinned and lifted herself from the grass, then pulled him up by the hand. "I guess you'll be bunking with me tonight. I always watch Perry Mason with my mama until she falls asleep."

"Seriously, who is he?"

# Chapter 6

Diego tried to hang but he couldn't. Christina had plenty of practice when it came time for her to stay awake and fall asleep only an hour after her mother. It seemed as though the late 1950's fictional lawyer had done the trick and put the dear prince under the spell of the Sand Man, with how he snored loudly with his head leaned back against the headboard. It had been that, a full stomach, his work schedule, and being cuddled underneath the thick comforter while sitting up that took him over. Christina wasn't too far behind. After an episode that aired in 1958, that she remembered line for line, she dozed off with her cheek pressing against Diego's chest.

When the alarm clock from Diego's room sounded, neither of them could hear it and Christina had forgotten to set the alarm on her phone. Even her force of habit hadn't gotten her awake, but the fear of oversleeping, however, did. Her eyes shot open and she leaned off of Diego, looked around for her phone and grabbed it off the nightstand on her side. When seeing what time it was, she panicked.

"Diego!" she shouted and slapped his bare arm. "Diego, get up!"

His back lifted off the headboard and his heart was pounding at her urgent tone. "What? Huh? What's wrong?" He wiped the corners of his mouth with the back of his hand while trying to remember where he was, yet all he could focus on was Christina scurrying around the room for her clothes and laptop. "What are you doing? What happened?"

"We overslept!" Finally, she shimmied her laptop and notepad out of her satchel and slammed them both onto the bed.

He whipped the covers back and hauled ass to his room. His morning regimen would have to be cut short because he had only 30 minutes to get to the trap and start his work day.

The day before, Christina had to learn how to use the coffee maker that Diego had apparently never used, and set an alarm on it so that it would brew her coffee automatically. She remembered and quickly traveled into the kitchen to pour herself a cup while her lecture was buffering. Instead of one cup, she poured two. Only the second was in a travel cup that she used quite often.

When Diego hurried out of his room, while pulling a black t-shirt over his head, he still had his toothbrush hanging out of the corner of his mouth. He patted his pocket for his keys, and she grabbed them off the bar, shuffled to him in her socks to give them to him, and handed him the cup of coffee she made.

"See you in a little bit," she hurried and said, and then pecked his cheek before he hit the door.

Diego jogged down the steps and only stopped to lean over the railing, just to spit out his toothpaste and continue brushing on the journey to his SUV. He had yet to stop and think of what had taken place the night before and just now. All that was on his mind was getting to the money.

When inside the Cadillac, he chugged down as much of the hot coffee as he possibly could to get himself to wake up a little more, and pulled his phone from his pocket. When he saw how many missed calls he had from Dena and the last two girls he saw before her, there was no question of if he would return their calls. Especially not right now. He backed out of his parking space while simultaneously taking his prepaid phone out of his glovebox. Missed calls and text messages galore. He'd have to wait until he stopped so that he could try and at least return a few of them.

Inside the trap, Ramone had his heavily tinted shades donning his face and held his head low while all of his men ran in and out with their supplies. Massaging his temple, he leaned back in his chair and rolled his head around on his shoulders. "Goddammit, where is Carrot Top?" he miserably grumbled. "I need one hell of a massage. No happy ending for me today. I need some magic fingers and a smooth voice."

"It's Tuesday," Diego mumbled as he jotted something down inside his father's composition notebook at the corner of his desk. "She doesn't come in until later."

Ramone slowly declined his head so that he could see his son and narrowed his eyes. "What're you drinking in that cup?" he asked him. "Please don't say it's liquor."

Diego lightly chuckled while opening his calculator app on his phone. "It's black coffee. Nasty as shit but it's doing the trick to keep me awake."

"Give it to me," Ramone said sternly. "Give it to me now and without backtalk."

Obediently, Diego handed his father the travel cup and swiped the notebook off the desk to take a closer look. Then he pulled up a chair on the furthest side and sat so that he could go down the row and add up profits.

Ramone slammed the cup down onto the table after guzzling it and took his eyes to his son. He studied him for a moment and noticed certain changes about him. How alert Diego was, how focused he was, and after what Black had told him about his own kid, he noticed how dedicated he was. "You fucked her, didn't you?" he suddenly asked.

"Hmm?" Diego mumbled. He wasn't worried about anything that had been said with his mind on getting the numbers right before his father had to go over them.

"You got you a piece of grown woman pussy and all of a sudden you come to work wide awake and bushy-tailed than a motherfucker."

Finally, Diego's head spun around to his father with his face contorted. "What?"

"See what I mean?" Ramone lightly chuckled. "You ain't heard shit I said. She got you all focused and deaf to bullshit. How'd it feel gettin' a taste of a real woman?"

"Daddy, what are you talkin' about?"

"Christina, Dutch! I'm talkin' about Christina! You fucked her, and now you're on your grown man shit."

Diego sucked his teeth and shook his head at the ignorance. "I hadn't smashed yet. She's not one of those who you can just dip into and run off on. Didn't think that I'd say this, but I actually like her. She's good people."

"She put somethin' in your veins, boy." Ramone leaned over his desk and stacked his forearms so that he could rest his head on them while continuing his conversation. He figured that it would ease his banging headache from his hangover a little. "I didn't tell you to come in here and go over the books, but you did that on your own. Shit, when it ain't nothin' to do, you ain't doin' somethin' right."

Diego slowly nodded as he made a star beside a line he found to be incorrect. Evidently, he was tuning his father out.

"How is she, though? For real. I know that she's a little pistol, and I know she's always busy, but what do you think about her?"

"If she stops being so damn mean, I think we can get a lot further. I mean, it's so much that I want to know about her. I just..."

Ramone lifted his head when noticing how his son was intensely studying the page. It wasn't until he flipped two pages and then a third when Ramone knew something was wrong. "What's up?"

"I need to go through this book," Diego mumbled. "Does everybody log in or...?"

"Sometimes I write in it, sometimes Black does, sometimes the guys write in it. Why?"

"Some stuff doesn't add up. Just give me until noon and I'll have something for you."

"Some shit like what?"

"Don't worry about it, daddy. I got it." Diego took off his shirt by pulling the back of it over his head, reached into what only looked like a pen cup and grabbed a cigarette from out of it along with a vintage silver lighter to light it. After blowing smoke from his lips, he said, "Are you going to sit there and look at me, or are you going to hand me a pen and another notebook?"

Baffled, Ramone opened a drawer on the side of him and rummaged through it so that he could fetch his son what he'd requested.

"I really hope you don't have to cut off any fingers today," Diego remarked. "Let's do the math and hope and pray like hell that you don't have to."

---

Christina was sitting in the bed Indian style while listening to her lecture and was twisting her hair all the while. She'd taken a shower in between courses and decided to twist her locks while they were still wet. That way, when she'd taken them down, they'd fly freely in curls.

There was a thunderous knock on the front door, and it startled her. She distinctively remembered giving Diego his keys, and it had been at least 4 hours since he'd been away. It couldn't have been him. She pressed pause on her video player and stood out of bed to stretch her clinging black tank top over her backside, and pull her black tights from between her legs. Then she shuffled to the front door in her dark gray knee high socks and stood on her tip-toes to peek out of the peephole. A fisheye view of a guy in a short sleeve white shirt with some type of delivery company scribbled on the front was before her. Her nose crinkled as she tried to think of what could've been delivered to the house. Reluctantly, she opened the door and greeted the man with a smile.

"Christina Jackson?" he asked her.

"That's me," she grinned.

He handed her the box and licked his lips while surveying her chubby figure in her clinging attire. "From Dutch C."

She accepted the long brown box and signed off on a receipt that lay near a large yellow bow.

"You, uh… live here alone?" he lowly asked.

"Oh, this isn't my home." She handed him the receipt and slammed the door in his face before he could pine over her so-called beauty and try to persuade her to connect with him later. Then she'd gone back into the room and hopped into bed so that she could press play on her laptop to complete her lecture. While listening to her instructor speak, she untied the bow on the box and lifted the lid. Underneath it, she found something that took her breath away. Diego sent her 14 yellow roses, but they weren't bunched together. They simply lay in a group. Across them had been a folded piece of paper that she opened and read.

*"I come in peace, Chrissy. Thank you for being here, and thank you for not being as mean as I thought you'd be to me. I'm actually enjoying my time with you. Please don't be mad but I'll be working very late tonight. I promise you that I'll make it up. See you way later on.*

*— Dutch."*

Her smile reappeared when she picked up a rose and scanned it, paying attention to every small detail of it. She lifted the blossomed rose to her nostrils and inhaled its perfumed scent, and closed her eyes to live in the moment. Never had anyone sent roses to her. Never had they taken the time to apologize for anything. It seemed as if the Diego she knew had done a complete 180-degree turn. He wasn't the same asshole he was when they met, and he wasn't the same guy that he was on Sunday night. Day by day he was transforming into somewhat of a charmer, and it made Christina want to know more about the road he walked before the contracts and before their first blowup. She figured that everyone only called him Dutch because his father's nickname on the streets was Duke. To her, there had to be more to it than that. Now that the ice between the two had long been broken, she could dig a little deeper and find out more about him. She could use the rest of her time wisely to do what they were supposed to do and mingle instead of just exist for a week. Honestly, she wished that the week would be extended. This version of Diego was someone she could keep.

—

By nightfall, shifts were being switched inside the trap and all of the young girls who worked in the "development room" had put on their clothes to leave and switch out with the next set of 4. Men had come in to count and report after a long day, but Diego wouldn't allow them to log in on the composition notebook he'd been scouring through. Instead, he had torn a page off of a notepad and set it on the desk so that they wouldn't confuse him. Even Ramone himself had been tired of going through the books and pulled his designer Gucci white tank top over his head to leave for the day.

"I got this," Diego assured him. "I'm not leaving until I figure out where the missing money and supplies are."

Ramone slapped his back and said, "I'm proud of you. But as soon as you figure out what the fuck—"

"I got it, pop. I'll call you as soon as I know what's up."

Ramone lightly nodded and grabbed a lit cigarette out of the ashtray before exiting the room.

"Duke," a young man said when he reached the living room. He sounded as though he had been in a panic.

Ramone threw up his hands and shuffled past the young one. "Take that shit to Dutch. I'm going home."

As instructed, he pushed past seven men who were trying to get their business out of the way and flattened his hands on the tabletop in front of Diego.

Diego himself hadn't realized what was happening around him with him being so consumed in numbers until a droplet of sweat splashed on the page he was reading. He looked up to find the young man there in distress. "What's up?" he asked him with a confused face.

The man shook his head and stressed, "Niggas is so called moving in on our turf, Dutch. Silk noticed that shit and I wasn't listening. A nigga named Puma got jumped a minute ago and they took what he had. They fucked him up so bad that somebody had to call an ambulance."

"Well, you get to whatever hospital where they took him and make sure he keeps his mouth closed. Tell the cops when they come that the niggas jumped him over a female. I'll get with Silk later about 'em. I got it."

The guy nodded and shook hands with him before pulling out a wad of money he earned and a single baggy of cocaine. "The name is Callahan," he said and scurried out of the trap.

Diego pushed the palms into his eyes until the sound of heavy plastic hitting the table distracted him. Quickly removing his hands, his eyes shot open to see what the hell else someone could've brought to him. To his surprise, there was a Glad container that had condensation inside of it, so he couldn't see what the contents were. Then there was another that had come down next to it along with a few plastic forks and spoons. Finally, he looked up to find Christina in front of the table as she pulled napkins out of her satchel. He stood and looked around as if her mother would pop up out of nowhere and give him a good tongue lashing for having her daughter in such a place. But his eyes had stopped on two older men in particular who had their orbs set on Christina's backside in her tights. He narrowed his eyes at them until they looked away, and grabbed her arms. "What are you doing here?" he asked her. "You shouldn't be in a place like this."

"Well, you're here, aren't you?" she sassed. "I can be here too, only for the moment."

"That's because this is a dangerous place and I'm a dangerous man, Christina. You realize that if we got raided, you'd be charged too? I don't want that for you."

"Then I guess you'd better scarf down what I brought you so that I can leave, knowing that you've eaten finally."

"For the sake of argument, I will. Sit."

She pulled out the chair on her side that Ramone left vacant, but Diego pulled her arm so that she could round the table, turned her around and sat in his seat while pulling her down onto his lap.

With an arm around her waist and the other hand multi-tasking by flipping the page, taking notes, then dropping the pen to pick up a fork so that he could feed his face, he was determined to hurry. The shower and bed at his home was calling his name. Suddenly a thought struck him in the midst of going over what he'd been told throughout the day and his numbers. He pecked her arm with his lips and asked, "How did you get here?"

"The bus," she lowly giggled.

"You mean to tell me you took that long ass walk from the condos to downtown and caught the bus?"

"Yup. All so that you can eat dinner. You told me that you were going to be late in your note, so I decided to make a little office visit. What are you working on?"

"Ledgers," he dryly mumbled. "Somebody's stealing money, product, territory and maybe something else. Shit just doesn't add up, but I'm trying to at least figure out where it's all going to."

"I'm sure that two eyes are better than one."

"Hell naw, Chrissy," he strongly opposed. "You're not even supposed to be in here. I can't let you get your hands dirty."

"Shut up. From what I can see, you have a list of names on that paper you're writing on, and on the other you're jotting down numbers and recording who made what total on a specific day. That's some good filtering. I have a calculator app. Give me the formula and I'm pretty sure I can have a solution for you."

"No, Christina."

"I'm not going to sit here and just look pretty for you," she complained as she lifted herself from Diego's lap and removed her satchel. "I come baring my own supplies anyway. Let me help."

"Fine," he grunted. "You better not tell anybody that I let you in on this."

"Who the fuck am I going to tell? I have no friends, remember?"

Almost 5 minutes after Christina pulled up a chair and sat it beside Diego so that they could share opposite pages, Christina noticed something when she'd gotten to a line that had Diego's name on it. Something was foul about it. She dug into her satchel at the furthest end of the table and retrieved the note that came with her flowers. She compared the handwriting and her jaw dropped at what she saw.

"Diego," she mumbled as he fed his face with her broccoli macaroni and cheese. "You didn't write this."

"Hmm?" He leaned over and stared the page she'd been looking at and found his name.

She laid the note he'd written for her on his side and pointed to the date at the top of it. "Look at how you write your numbers," she explained. "Then look at the ones in the ledger. The D in your signature doesn't even closely resemble the D in your signature on my note. Someone else wrote this."

He squinted his eyes and thought about it for a second. For the last few weeks he had been signing the ledgers and putting in what he earned, just like everyone else. However, Christina was right. What he was looking at wasn't what he'd written. It made him go back to the first page for the month and double check what he logged and noticed that only a few pages had his actual signature on them. If someone was setting him up, maybe they were setting the others up too, but who? His eyes then shot up to the desk across the room where the sheet of paper he tore off the notepad had been sitting underneath the lamp. "Chrissy, get that paper over there," he ordered. "Fuck what we're counting right now. We need to start on that dough over there." He watched on as she obeyed and gathered what he needed. "Get the bands of money and shit too. Trust me; it's only gonna take about an hour. Right now we need to go through signatures in this book and compare 'em to signatures on this page. Somebody is cooking some shit up and my daddy ain't gonna like this shit."

"What do we need to do right now, though?" she asked she sorted through all of the drugs and money she piled onto the table. "What's more important? Do we count or do we do the signatures? I think we can cut through time if we divide the duty."

"Right. You compare signatures and write down the names and dates that are off. We'll compare dates from my original notes afterward. Right now, I'll double check the work."

Christina nodded and took the ledger from Diego and twisted it around to make note of what he'd asked of her, but by the time she was done and they looked over everything, it didn't make sense. According to the books, he, along with six others, had been stealing from Ramone. It's when he checked the dates that he had to stop focusing and sit back in the chair with misty and rage-filled eyes.

"What's wrong?" Christina innocently asked.

Diego raised his tired and sleepy body out of the chair and noticed that it was close to 1AM. He'd been working all day on something he should've caught on to over 12 hours prior. He got a new pack of cigarettes out of the carton his father sent for 14 hours ago and opened his second pack for the day. After he lit it and inhaled his smoke, a tear trickled down his cheek. He leaned his head back and released his smoke slowly, then quickly took another pull afterward. "Some things are hard as fuck to accept," he mumbled.

"Like what?"

"Like the man who helped to raise me and kept my half-breed ass out of trouble, stealing from my damn daddy." He softly banged on his chest— specifically on a large gothic styled C that had been tattooed over his left peck— and sadly said, "For mi familia. All or none." He lightly chuckled then and turned to a worried Christina, who was a bit taken aback by his sudden shock and sadness. "My daddy told me that once. He said that everybody had a place in this family, but when he finds out that his right hand had been feeding off of him... he's gonna lose it."

Christina's hand slowly drew up to her mouth at his statement, but Diego wasn't done just yet.

"I've been wondering how or why my mama hadn't been out on the streets yet, and how it is that she's able to post pictures of her shopping sprees on Instagram. And at first, I thought that either she was stealing other people's pictures or that she took out a loan. Nah. It's because he's been siphoning money for her rat ass."

"Don't jump to any conclusions now, Diego," she reasoned. "How do you know for sure? I mean, I know you two aren't fond of one another, but you got to have solid proof before you get innocent people whacked off."

"The proof is in the books, babe. He was stealing and taking money on the dates that we willingly handed shit over to him. Coincidentally, they were on days that my daddy went out of town. Then on the next day, or the day after, my mama's stupid ass freely posts photos of parties and shopping trips. That ain't odd to you?"

"What's odd to me is how she's showing that this man is stealing knowing that if her ex-husband found out that she'd be killed for having someone on the inside give her money that she's not entitled to. I strongly believe that: yes she's a gold digger, yes she's probably sleeping with him for her funds... but she doesn't know where the money is coming from. It doesn't add up. And since when does a gold digger ask a baller where they get their money? Just think about it. It may kill you to save her life, but this is on him. Yea, she has consequences for accepting your dad's right hand man's money in the first place when she's supposed to be cut off, but I don't think snitching her out is the way to go."

Diego reached out to her and grabbed the lining of her spandex tank top and pulled her in for a kiss on the lips. When he drew away, he grumbled, "I like that you're the voice of reason. Keep doing that. I needed that."

"Anytime." She smiled and pecked his lips. "Can we leave now? I'm sure everybody has had a long day, and I'm tired as hell. I don't think your dad needs to hear this until tomorrow. Reenergize and call a meeting in the morning or something. We don't want to oversleep."

"You got that shit right. I almost dozed off at a stop light this morning. If it wasn't for you thinking about me staying awake, I probably would have. Look who earned her place at the number one spot."

"It was effortless," she giggled. "I'm pretty sure that the other woman has her good qualities as well."

"Yea, but she's going to have to walk on water and save souls to beat you out."

"Either that or have voodoo pussy."

"You're so corny," he laughed.

# Chapter 7

After a nice shower and watching the recording of Perry Mason, the pair dozed off while being tangled within each other's arms. Diego lay on his back with one of Christina's legs crossing over his, and her cheek was mashed against his collarbone. While his eyes had been glued to the ceiling, he hadn't realized that she wasn't faintly snoring. The sky's soft blue and purple rays shown through the drapes and were welcomed against the walls of the room where they lay, meaning that it had to be between 5AM and 6AM. He hadn't realized that either. His thoughts were consumed with his honorary uncle, Black. How long had he been biting Ramone's hand? How long had he been giving Markiesha money to stay afloat? It just didn't make sense to him, but the proof was right in front of his eyes. How on earth would he break the news to his father and the others who could've possibly had their fingers chopped off because of his insubordination? His jaw tightened and his nostrils flared. It was angering and hurting him all over again.

Christina stretched her neck and kissed the underpart of his chin, and his goatee tickled her lips. "Why are you awake?" she hoarsely asked him. "It's still on your mind, isn't it?"

He quietly replied with another question. "What's your favorite color, Christina?"

"Yellow," she softly chuckled. "What's yours?"

"Red. What's your favorite food?"

"All soul food."

"I like Italian. Favorite song?"

"Beautiful by India.Arie."

"Switch Up by Big Sean. If you could go anywhere in the world, where would it be and why?"

"Back to Dreamland," she giggled.

He gave her a pat on her backside and a smile finally stretched across his face.

"For real. I would want to go to Cairo. I want to see the ancient majestic beauty up close and personal. How about you?"

"I don't know. Never really thought of it before. I'll get back to you on that one."

She stroked his bare chest and studied the hills in his skin when trying to form the right words for her next statement. The last thing she wanted, given the situation, was to upset him any further. "Diego, you didn't sleep at all last night, did you?"

He flexed his jaw instead of answering. To be betrayed by the single person who helped his own father build a dynasty— and who helped rebuild it after his mother tore through it and had workers jumping ship— was something that squeezed his heart. Black was the perfect example of a loyal friend, but he turned out to be nothing but a wolf in sheep's clothing.

Christina had reached up to his cheek, and she loving stroked his baby face as she nuzzled her nose in the crook of his neck. "Just try and get an hour of sleep before you go in to work," she whispered and kissed his neck softly. "You don't want to go in there looking a mess when you mean business."

Diego grabbed the small of her back and tightened the trim of her shorts within his fist to bring her over his lap. With his free hand, he tangled his fingers within her locks and pulled her face into his. He had given her the most passionate kiss that he could muster, and he hadn't wanted to stop. He was tired of controlling himself.

She didn't mind with the way her hips slowly gyrated over his pelvis until he was rock hard underneath her. The two had gotten lost in their kiss. Both of his hands had gone to her cheeks inside of her shorts, and he grabbed them, smacked them and parted them.

"I want these off," he whispered between kisses. "Please, Christina. Take them off."

"You said please," she grinned and gave him one last peck on the lips before sliding off.

Diego got out of bed and briskly traveled into his room for condoms he knew he had but prayed he hadn't run through as of yet. After finding one in his nightstand, he slipped it on and pulled his shorts back up so that Christina wouldn't think that he was too anxious.

She was in the bed and under the covers when he entered, and he stopped in his tracks to take in the sight of her in nothing but her bra, anticipating his skills. Her shoulder was hitched as she clenched the covers underneath her breast for dear life. He made his way over to the bed and pulled back the covers back with ease before situating himself between her legs. To distract her, he pressed his lips softly against hers and pulled her legs to bring her down in bed a few inches away from the headboard. He could feel her slightly shiver against him, so he didn't want to take things too fast with her.

Her arms wrapped around his neck and before she could give a thought toward opposing, he pushed himself inside of her. She gasped at his entrance and shut her eyes to explore the moment. Though Diego kept his promise and was very gentle with her, every pump felt as if his dick would break with how it bent due to her tightness. His motions quickened, and Christina couldn't catch her breath. He had to stroke her in circles to get her to adjust to his size quicker than usual. When her legs wrapped around his waist, he knew he had her and that he could control their escapade the way he would any other time.

Just as he pulled out, his cellphone rang in his pants, and it was his mother's ringtone. He looked over his strewn jeans and tilted his head at it. Why would she be calling this early in the morning?

Christina kissed his earlobe and relaxed her head on the pillows below. "Work is calling," she softly said.

"No, it's my mama," he mumbled. "What the fuck?"

"Should you pick it up?"

"Fuck her," he grunted and forced himself deep inside of Christina.

She squealed though she hadn't stopped him. Instead, she clutched his neck and hung on with everything she had. His lower back was putting her midsection to the test. Her toes curled against his flexing back muscles and she hadn't held in her cries of passion. Diego loved her love faces. In fact, they made him bite his bottom lip and stroke her deeper just to see if she'd submit. Further he pushed and grabbed the trim of her bra with his teeth to pull it down as far as it could go so that he could twirl his tongue over her erect nipple, and suckle on it while holding it between his teeth.

The only thing to stop him was the sound of his father's ringtone. His head popped up and whipped over to his jeans a few feet away from the bed. "What the fuck?" he said in disbelief. Then he looked down at Christina, who had caged her bottom lip between her teeth. "Do you think they know what's going on?"

"I don't know," she huffed. "Maybe. All I know is that I didn't want you to stop. Go answer for your folks."

He cautiously pulled his dick away from her and had gone over to his jeans. By the time he retrieved his phone out of his thick denim pants, his father had hung up. He clicked on the notification that told him that he had a missed call just to quickly call him back. After sitting on the side of the bed, he took out his pack of cigarettes that he had taken from the trap and lit one. While waiting for Ramone, he blew his smoke and tried to gather as much courage as he could to tell him what he found if need be.

"Come get your mama," Ramone tiredly said. "I gotta get to the office in a little bit, and she needs to sleep off the sauce."

"I'm not drunk!" Markiesha shouted in the background. "You just gonna call Diego over here like he's my fuckin' handler? He's my *son*! He can't move me! I'm a grown ass woman!"

"Come and get her ass before I have to slap the shit out of her again, Dutch. You know I will."

He fixed his mouth to say something but his father had already hung up the phone and left him there to lean his forehead against the LCD of his cell.

"What's wrong?" Christina sympathetically asked him from over his shoulder.

"I need to go and play a game of Daycare with my folks," he mumbled. "He thinks my mama is drunk but she says she's not."

"Well... go and do what you need to do. And add on your plate that you owe me when you get back. I don't care if I'm in the middle of a lecture or not. Give it to me."

He peaked over his shoulder with his eyebrows pressed tightly together. "Really?"

"Really. Now I see why you're so cocky."

He shook his head and grabbed his jeans from the floor to slide them on. Before buttoning them, he reached inside his underwear and pulled off his condom and tossed it into the wastebasket beside the bed. Then he gave her another deep kiss that promised her that they weren't anywhere near finished with what they started. After washing his hands, he jogged down the stairs to his SUV and checked his cellphone once more. One of the girls he had a threesome with had sent him a text message hours ago that said that he really needed to return his phone calls. She had also sent him a photo of a pregnancy test. It made him stop at the grill of his Cadillac and look up the steps as if Christina was standing there over the railing to wave him goodbye. No, he hadn't replied to the girl's text, but he sent one to Angel so that he could make under-the-table arrangements to get her situation taken care of.

—

Diego could hear every gauntlet his parents had slapped one another with, metaphorically, when he stepped out of his SUV on the street. His own reserve rooted him to the curb, and his feet wouldn't allow him to move any further than where he was. The last time he was able to step foot into his father's Flowood, Mississippi villa was when he was 13 years old, and he had dropped a magazine and had to backtrack to pick it up; the day his mother called the police and asked for an escort away from Ramone. He shut his eyes tight and trudged on up the slim and curved walkway away from the curb, and used the key he never took off of his keyring to enter.

If any visitor entered Ramone's foyer, they'd see that every detail had been addressed with the herringbone pattern in the wood flooring and would be amazed by the majestic 48-foot ceilings. The formal dining room where his parents were throwing insult after insult had picture windows with designer fixtures behind the satin drapes. A beautiful place, but it wasn't so beautiful to Diego because of things, like the shouting match in front of him, that had been transpiring since he was just a boy. If the coral colored walls could talk, they'd spill every secret the Caraway family had, and they'd most definitely tell the Mr. and Mrs. how much their son couldn't stand to step inside of such a beautiful yet hellish place.

"*Shut the fuck up*!" Diego roared over the bickering pair. "Why can't y'all sit in the same goddamn place without fuckin' fightin'? Oh, but you're supposed to be teaching me about marriage and life lessons, right?"

"Make sure you don't marry a bitch who's only after your money," Ramone said to him with his chest heaving. "That's all I wanted from you, which is why we did a damn good screening of all the girls we brought to you. I did it so you wouldn't end up with a money hungry bitch like the one that's standing in front of me." He turned away from Markiesha and pressed his forearm into the faux cherry wood finish mantel of the fireplace, and rested his forehead against his arm. Even Diego could tell that his parents were clawing that badly at one another to have his father turn his back to her and wear such a sad and angry expression on his face.

Markiesha tried to wipe away her running mascara from her cheeks, but all she did was smear it more than it had been. "You keep thinking that I'm lying to you but I'm not," she said with a shaky voice. "All I want is my fucking family back."

"You never had one," Ramone informed her between closed teeth.

"I did, and I didn't see it until—"

"Until you sent my ass to jail for domestic abuse?" Ramone yelled as he whirled around to her. "Or was it until you fucked every last one of the niggas that was there with me since day one? Or was it when you damn near tore me in half financially? Bitch, answer me!"

"Daddy, stop," Diego intervened, as soon as his father took a step toward Markiesha and raised his hand. "Markiesha, when did you even get here?"

"She came almost two-fucking-hours ago." Ramone pulled out a tall back chair that was pushed up to his shiny cherry wood table and plopped down in it. "She wanted to fuck, we fucked, and when it was time to go, she turned on the damn water works. I should've never fucked you twenty-three years ago, and none of this would be happening."

"Hold on now, pop—"

"Ain't no hold on. You're the best thing to come out of this situation. You're the only good damn thing this bitch has ever done in her fucking life. Fuck that hoe."

"Diego, tell him," Markiesha pleaded. "Tell him that we can still be a family. I'm going to be tied to you forever because you're my son, and it's the same between you and him. Please! Tell him!"

"No offense, Markiesha, but you don't have the best reputation for me to defend you," Diego reasoned. "I'm confused as to why you'd be over here begging for something that you lost almost ten years ago. Actually, longer than that if you want to count how long it'd been since you two even slept in the same room."

"Son, I lo—"

"Easy, Markiesha," he warned her. "I saw a girl weep desperately over her mother while she was trying to get her to breathe again, and all I could think was that I would *never* do that for you because of all of the fucked up shit that you've done."

"What?"

"It's true. And earlier tonight I was trying to figure out how in the hell you've been posting so much on your Instagram, but you're supposedly broke. That's before I noticed that somebody had their hands in my daddy's vault."

Ramone's head popped up at his son and his eyes had gone wide at the unobvious deception.

"Now I'm trying to figure out— with all of the men you've had executed because of your voodoo— why Uncle Black?"

"Black?" Ramone mumbled.

"You come here begging, slinging snot and tears for a family, but you're fucking my godfather? How long has it been?"

"We're not fucking," she sniffled. "How did you know that he was giving me money? He told me that he wouldn't tell anybody."

"He didn't. My daddy's *books* told me."

Markiesha's face fell and her jaw damn near hit the floor. Her stomach knotted and the room began to spin around her. Markiesha had to waddle over to the mantle and grab on to it. She blinked multiple times to try and understand what her son had said. With her hand on the stomach of her black sheer flowing gown, she turned her head to her son and slowly shook it. "Nobody's that fucking stupid to steal from your daddy, boy. *Especially* Black. He knows better. You got to come a lot harder than that to convince me otherwise."

"Oh, so you *didn't* know?"

"Didn't know *what*?" she cried. "Diego, you're not making any sense, and you're scaring me!"

"He's been cooking my daddy's books to provide for your greedy ass! That's what I'm saying."

Markiesha viciously shook her ringlet curls so much so that she shook the bobby pin loose that kept her stylish swoop in place. It fell over her right eye and gave her a very crazed look. She hugged herself as if she was trying her best not to have a nervous breakdown, and slowly fell to her knees as Ramone rose out of his seat. "He wouldn't do that," she mumbled. "No. *No!* Black would never take from Ramone. Ramone pays him a salary. All that money came from his pocket. That's what it is. You just looked at the books incorrectly; that's all. He's too much of a good friend to Ramone. He wouldn't do that." She burst into laughter and palmed her forehead. "That's it. That's exactly what it is." She looked up and over at her son with a beaming smile on her face. "You just overlooked something, Diego. Black is honest. He's a very honest man."

"I don't know who the fuck you're trying to convince— me or you— but his handwriting is the only one that matches all of those forged ass signatures in the notebook."

"He wouldn't do that to your dad!"

"I had a hard time believing it too, but it's what happened."

Ramone ripped away from the dining room and had gone into his master bath where he left his phone on the countertop, and called his old friend. After telling him to meet him at the trap, he grabbed his keys off the dresser and headed for the front door.

"Get your ass up, Kiesha," he said when he stopped in his foyer. "I'm not done with your begging ass so you'd better be here when I get back."

"Ramone—"

"Bitch, I said you better be here!" he screamed at her. "And if you're not, the police looking for me is going to be the least of both of our worries. Dutch, let's go."

Diego shook his head at his crying mother and left her in front of the fireplace. What his father was going to do to her was none of his business after today. He felt sorry for her, but he'd have to leave it there.

# Chapter 8

Every last man on the payroll filled the living and dining area of the apartment where Ramone and his son conducted their business, and no one knew what had been happening in order for Ramone to call an emergency meeting. Almost as if to mock them in a way, Diego spoke up so that his father didn't have to. "Does anybody know why you're here?"

The sight of Ramone sharpening his ax while sitting on the edge of the coffee table frightened some of his foot soldiers to the point where they didn't want to speak up at all. He was an angry man who sat there in his wife beater— his veins popping out of his bare arms and his eyes red as ever. The others knew that someone would be missing limbs.

Silk shimmied in between two young men and said, "Obviously somebody's been fuckin' with Duke's cash flow. But who is it? Step forward. Now you're fuckin' with *my* money. It may be dead out there because it's Wednesday, but we still grind no matter what. Who did it?"

"Why?" Ramone mumbled as he lowered his ax and stared at the floorboards. "Why did it have to be the only nigga that I trusted my own kid with? Why did it have to be the nigga that I broke bread with when I only had one piece?"

Black leaned off the wall and looked down at his best friend of almost 30 years and pressed his brows together. "You sayin' that I stole from you?"

"No," Diego opposed. "He *knows* that you've been cookin' the books for my mama. We just want to know why. And we want to know why you would frame me and six other niggas just make her live the lavish life that was taken away from her. Do you not understand that we all could've been maimed because of what you did?"

"Hold up. You're gonna stand here and tell me to my face that... man, watch out." He approached Diego, but he should've been paying attention to his boss.

With one swing, Ramone took off Black's forearm and every man in the living room scrambled around to get out of the way. The ax was only lodged inside of Black's ribs for a split second before it had fallen off and landed onto the floor. Shortly after, Black dropped to his knees. He was screaming at the top of his lungs from the pain and agony while trying to figure out if what just happened had really taken place.

His chest heaving and all, Ramone fished his phone from his pocket and dialed 9-1-1. The only thing Diego could do was stand there and stare at the man on the floor who was crying real tears. Diego knew that Black had gotten what he deserved but could he had done something to stop it?

"Yea, the motherfucker ran off. A crazy lookin' motherfucker," Ramone said into his phone. "He must've been on drugs, or either the nigga that got his shit whacked owed him somethin'."

"Get him out of here!" Diego shouted, just after his father hung up the phone and after he snapped out of his trance. "Drag him to the plaza or the parking lot and haul all ass! Somebody make sure ain't no blood on the stairs, and get those girls out of the room and have them clean this shit up! Y'all move!" He then grabbed his father's arms to shake him and to take Ramone's eyes off of Black. "Daddy, you gotta leave!" he shouted at him while others shuffled around to do as they were told. "You gotta go! Get the fuck out of here so that you won't be here when they get here! I'm sure Black is gonna keep his damn mouth closed."

"You were mi familia!" Ramone growled at Black while a few men threw a sheet over him to roll him up in it. "I took your right arm off because you took the right part of my soul, motherfucker! You stole from *me*? I'm the motherfuckin' Duke! You took from *me*? Nigga, I fed you! I took care of your fuckin' family!"

"Daddy! Go!" Seeing his father in such horrible shape was going to haunt Diego for the rest of his life. To see him so red in the face with cloudy eyes and having saliva fly all over the place as he spoke. Black should've been dead for what he did, but at least he left with only one arm for lying and stealing.

Diego pushed his father out of the door and had someone to follow him to his car and back to Flowood just to make sure that he made it home without turning back and finishing Black off. His head panged from all of the drama, but he'd have to get used to it since he was gearing up to take on half the business in a little more than two weeks from then.

—

After the police left and swept the area thoroughly, Diego had finally dragged himself away from the projects. It was nearing 8PM and he didn't want to look at another number, whether it was on a scale or on paper, or even if it was a bill. He needed a release. It wasn't until he was on the freeway headed back to his condo that he realized that the business was why his father had a daily double dose of scotch and tequila. Quite often, to keep himself calm, Ramone would sip lean and Diego saw that it would be fit to do the same. Everything happened so quickly that he was trying his best to make sense of it all, but he couldn't. What Ramone did was follow the laws of the savage business that is the drug game. Diego had to come to grips with it.

When he shut off the ignition in his parking space, he rested his forehead against the steering wheel but was disturbed by his cellphone blaring in his pocket. It was Angel. He'd sent Diego a text message that said, *"The bitch got taken care of. You owe me five stacks, my nigga. I had to bribe that bitch to get that abortion. Good thing she agreed to take the abortion money out of the bribe after I put that good wood to her. She shouldn't be bothering you anymore."*

Diego turned off the screen and banging his head against the steering wheel. He just wanted to be left alone and spend some real time with Christina for a change.

By the time he dropped his keys onto his nightstand and had taken his shirt off, he could hear the clomp of Christina's sneakers against the hardwood floor in the hall. He turned around and tilted his head at his bedroom door to wait for her to turn the corner. Sure enough, she had, but she had her rolling luggage in tow, and it made him panic. He jetted out of his room and caught the handle of the luggage so that she couldn't move it any further. "Where're you going?" he asked her.

Her eyes kissed every bit of his upper half, but she had to go back to being the Christina that she was before she let her walls down for him. "It's Wednesday," she remarked. "My mom has her surgery in the morning. I don't want to risk oversleeping or having to bother you to get up so that you can take me to the hospital. Buses don't run that early out that way. It's cool. I'll be back on Friday evening."

"Chrissy, you can't leave me now... I mean..." Diego pursed his lips and stroked his goatee so that he could get his words in order. Could he seriously show her the selfish side of him, or could he be the prince of charm that he had become quite accustomed to being in the last few days. "Just... tell your mama that I said hello. Okay?"

A small smile splashed onto Christina's face, and she stood on the tips of her toes inside of her sneakers to peck Diego's chin. "Text me, okay?"

"Yea," he merely mumbled.

"Don't look so sad," she giggled. "I'm not running away. I'll be back. I'm *obligated* to, remember?"

"So that's the only reason you're coming back? Because of the contract?"

"No, silly. I'm coming back for you. Believe it or not, I've actually grown to like you, and I love the way we sleep together. You're so warm and... I don't know," she shrugged. "I'll be back, okay?"

He faintly nodded and helped her take her belongings down to a waiting cab in the parking lot. After opening the back door for her, he grabbed her arm and pulled her into a kiss that she hadn't been expecting.

When Christina pulled back, she had to catch her breath. Diego was putting the heat on her, and she hadn't known if he was being clingy because there was a rift in the family or if it was because he really wanted her. Either way, she loved it. She just didn't know how to say it. Besides, he'd still have to spend a whole seven days with someone else. Christina couldn't take the chance of getting involved with him and then turn around and lose a careless game to someone who turned out to be the Saint of Mississippi. That in itself was the single reason that she couldn't open herself to a certain extent for him or even mouth the fact that she wanted him.

---

The next morning, Christina woke up to her phone buzzing on the arm of the couch in her mother's hospital room at 4:45AM. It was a picture message from Diego. The sad expression he wore on his face made her smile, but with the dark circles around his eyes she knew that he hadn't slept at all. She leaned off the pile of pillows she stacked and realized that her mother was having her vitals checked by a nurse.

"Good morning," Regina greeted her.

"Morning, mommy," she weakly smiled as she rubbed her eyes.

"That phone of yours has been scootin' further and further toward the edge of that arm, and I was scared that it was gonna fall on over." Regina giggled and it made her daughter shake her head at her.

Christina scrolled upward in her thread of texts from Diego to confirm that he didn't sleep.

*"I miss you, Chrissy."*

*"Are you asleep on me?"*

*"I think you are."*

*"Now I know you are."*

*"It would be a lot easier if you were here with me, so I can sleep too. But I know your mama is more important."*

*"Do you think that it's possible for me and my mama to have a relationship after all of this time?"*

*"Here goes nothing. I'm gonna call her ass and hope that she ain't on no beggin' type shit at this hour. Shit, I ain't got shit else better to do."*

*"CHRISTINA!"*

*"I wish you were awake. I'm gonna sad face the fuck outta you for fallin' asleep on me, girl. Do you know who I am? I'll do it. You don't think I would?"*

*"My dad's not picking up the phone, but I talked to my mama for a little bit. I'll tell you about that tomorrow. He's gonna be pissed because I told everybody not to work today. I ain't in no condition to go in, and I know he ain't either. Damn, I miss you."*

*"You missed a damn good episode of Perry Mason. This clown got murdered. Seriously, he was a real clown."*

Christina covered her mouth to hold in her laugh. He must've had it bad for her, she thought.

"I see you enjoyed your time with your young prince," Regina said with a grin. "I don't see why you're here and not with him."

Christina rolled her eyes away from the screen and over to her mother who was sitting straight up in the bed. "Don't question my loyalty, Regina Jackson," she said smartly. "I did what you wanted me to do which was go out and enjoy life. I'm doing that. But there was nothing in a clause that said I couldn't be at my mother's side while she has a very life-changing or threatening surgery."

"Still, I'm glad to see you smile."

Christina finally replied to Diego's long list of messages, and it was something she was sure to set him off. *"For your information, I've seen that episode, thank you. Season four, episode seven. It's really called Case of the Clumsy Clown. By the way, I know that you didn't sleep last night. Don't expect to leave the house at all on Friday. When I'm done seeing about my mama, I'm going to come and take care of you."*

*"Yes, baby,"* he replied. *"Take care of me good, girl."*

Regina noticed her daughter's smile widen, and it rubbed off on her. "So what's he like?" she asked aloud. "What's he really like? I know that after your first date you said that he was everything but a child of God."

"He's so different," Christina sang. "I thought that he would be the same idiot who accused me of being a lesbian, but he's not. He's a gentleman, he's thoughtful, and I seem to intimidate him. Mama, he kissed me, but I had to take control for him to stop shaking so dang hard."

"You're an intimidating something or other," Regina laughed. "I'd be scared to even touch you."

"That's the thing." Christina tucked her legs underneath her bottom and swiped her curly tresses behind her ears when thinking of all of the good qualities she found in Diego. She was all too excited to share them. "When we sleep together... he makes me feel like I don't have a thing to worry about when I get up the next morning. And when we're alone, we just have fun together, mama. He's not an uptight, arrogant prick when we're eating or just watching TV. And the other day? He was busy like crazy, but it didn't stop him from sending me yellow flowers and a cute little note to tell me that he'd be in late. That's not in his character. It's like he's changing for life... but he's changing for me too."

"Does he know that your favorite color is yellow?"

"He does now," she laughed. "He didn't know at the time, though."

"I'd say it took someone who wasn't so submissive or something he wasn't used to, to come along and put him in his place."

"Oh, mama... he holds me so close." Thinking of it made Christina hold herself and slowly mash her back against the cheap leather cushion of the couch. "He holds me as if he doesn't want to let me loose. Like he's gonna lose me at any given moment. Especially when we sleep together. It's like he's afraid to fall asleep because I'm gonna run away." She took a deep breath and smiled at her mother. "But I can't hold on to him like that."

"What?" Regina shrieked. Even the nurse who was listening to the woman's lungs had taken out her earbuds at that statement. "And why not?"

"Let's face it. He has to spend time with another woman in a few days. Maybe he's going to go over there and do all of these things with her. Maybe she's going to turn out to be better than me somehow, and I can't risk the chance of being hurt, mama. You know I can't trust anything. I don't expect a single thing from anyone who isn't under our roof. If I don't expect it, then it won't be a surprise when it doesn't fall through."

"Chrissy, come on. The boy is giving you the most of him through this thing."

"The funny thing is that I don't know if he's acting or if he's being real with me. Honestly, I want him all to myself, but I have to be fair. I have to be fair to the both of us. At the end of the day, him dating me is all a game."

"Then play to win," the nurse remarked as she worked her neck at Christina. "If I had a man to hold me the way you said he does, I wouldn't even come close to letting him out of my sight. You better grab him and not let him go."

Christina cocked a brow at the tall and shapely African American woman in her dark blue scrubs. Maybe the woman had a point, but still Christina wasn't willing to take that chance.

—

Diego stepped out of the shower and wrapped a towel around his waist. It was nearing 7AM, and he figured the hot water would help put him to sleep. Unfortunately, it hadn't. The young man was restless. After dressing in a black Dickie button up and dark blue denim shorts he made his way to the projects to oversee the girls who had been cooking up his father's product, collect money that had been brought in a few hours prior, and correct the books. He made a delivery to Silk and told him that he'd have to let the others know to come and get work from him if they needed it, and reminded him to keep records. Afterward, he took a 12-minute trip to Flowood and hadn't said a word to his father when he deposited what little money he had collected for Ramone's profit inside of his vault. On his way out, he noticed his father's big and bulky body hanging halfway off the couch. His head had been in Markiesha's lap.

She'd changed out of her black chiffon gown and was clad in a football Jersey Ramone had custom designed for the SEC Mississippi college team. She sat there softly stroking Ramone's long sideburns and broke into a small smile. "You get your sideburns from your daddy," she said hoarsely. "Shit, I'm glad that you took after him. If you were only my son, you'd be ugly as hell. Makeup could only get me so far back in the day. I don't even remember what my original nose looked like. I've had it changed four or five times."

"Why are you here, Markiesha?" Diego asked her as he leaned against the entryway of the sitting room.

"I'm here because I fucked up and now I have to fix it." She looked up at her son and Diego furrowed his brows. Her eyes were red and puffy, her skin was oily, her lips weren't as big as he thought they were, and she hadn't had any eyebrows. It was almost as if he was looking at a completely different person. He couldn't even remember what she looked like without makeup, and it helped him come to the conclusion that he'd never seen her without base and bronzer. "I wanted money," she sniffled, "but I never thought that Black would be as crazy to steal it from Ramone's pocket. Yea, I fucked a few of his homeboys, but that was to get attention from him that I didn't have to even ask for. Yea, me fucking them tore his empire apart, but that wasn't my intention. Now look at this, Dutch. I done fucked around and turned brothers against one another when I didn't even ask Black for a single damn handout. It damn near killed Duke last night. All he did was drink and curse, drink some more, tear up his room and drink again. He finally passed out about an hour ago. I'd never seen your daddy cry." She slowly shook her head and tucked a few of her curls behind her ear. In doing so, she revealed a fresh scar on her jaw that was newly healing. It wasn't there before Diego left her in front of the fireplace. His father must've slugged her a few hours ago. "I know one thing, though. No matter what we've been through and no matter how much we act like we can't stand each other... I'm going to always love this man. I just don't know how to show him to his face. Shit, if he was awake, I wouldn't be this affectionate toward him." A few tears spilled over, and she leaned down to kiss his cheek gently.

Instead of asking questions, Diego left the house and had more on his mind. His thoughts didn't confuse him any. He had it understood that he was the true product of his mother and father. He was an entitled bastard because his father was considered a king, and any and everything he wanted he received. He was vain and inconsiderate because of his mother cherishing material things and her looks. And together neither of them could express their love for one another. It was quite clear that Markiesha wouldn't have been a married woman or would've been exposed to better things had she not brought a child into the world without Ramone. Diego thought of the experiment his father put him through for a bride and figured it was because he wanted him to make better decisions without any fuck ups along the way. But it was still up to Diego to learn from it and to choose wisely while under the supervision of a man who had seen and done almost everything.

The only thought that washed away the others was Christina. She knew how to show genuine love. He saw it the day she tried to save her mother. She showed real concern by constantly keeping tabs on her. He could learn from her. "Ain't no second place," he mumbled after shutting the door to his SUV and buckled his seatbelt. "She's mine."

# Chapter 9

Christina was fixing her mother's hair wrap almost an hour after the nurses had brought her back to her room. The only thing she had been concerned with was how well the surgery had gone and was pleased when they told her that it was a success. They'd have to monitor her heart rate for another week before releasing her. It didn't matter to Christina. The hospital and her job was on the same bus line. She could travel to them both without there being an issue. With Regina being comfortable and settled, it was time for her to take a nap after her lecture. Just after she laid down on the couch and shut her eyes, her throw blanket was raised a few inches above her chest. Seeing as how her hands were tucked inside of her armpits, she wondered who could take such an advance, and opened her eyes. The figure before her almost made her scream, but she hadn't. She couldn't stop herself from quickly leaning off the leather or from throwing her arms around his neck.

Diego smiled over her shoulder and squeezed her.

"You smell so good," she quietly said.

He drew away and sat beside her while propping her feet over his lap. "I brought you something," he said with a smile.

She rolled her eyes. "I told you that I have my own money."

"Shut up and let me do stuff for you," he lowly demanded. He handed her a small white bag and rubbed her bare leg underneath the covers. While she rummaged through it, he looked up at the hospital bed and grimaced. "Chrissy, you got her sleeping on hospital covers? That's just nasty."

"What?" she questioned as she took a small brown teddy bear out of the bag.

"You don't know who didn't want to wash them sheets the right way. You need to get her some covers of her own. She's gonna go home and have some type of rash when this is over. Twelve-hundred thread count. That shit's nice."

"Diego... shut your face. We're good."

"Oh, and that ain't for you." He yanked the bear out of her hand and pushed her legs out of his lap so that he could get up and take it over to Regina's side table.

"Rudeness," she hissed.

"How'd you sleep?" he asked her as he pulled a chair over to the couch where he left her. "I'd say you slept damn good in order not to reply to my messages until this morning."

"We need to talk."

"We do. I've decided that I'm not going to spend a week with Dena. I don't need her. Whatever she has is something that I'm not interested in. Chrissy, I've never been interested in just one woman. And I think I know why that is. It's because I didn't want a torn home like the one my folks have. But in you, I see hope. I mean, look. You've been taking care of your mama for years. You believe in longevity. I need that. I need that solid shit that you have."

"Diego," she huffed. Even though what he'd said moved her, she had to stick to her guns. She reached out and took his hands into her own and almost melted when he delivered soft kisses to each of her palms. She only hoped that what she had to say was well received and taken into consideration. "I like being with you, I really do. You're going to breach your contract if you don't spend your week with her. Besides, I can't allow myself to get hurt. I'm on a straight and narrow path that won't allow me to step off of it. I have my life planned out and—"

"You know, the first time I heard your bio I said that I wasn't willing to take care of anyone's parents?" he asked her. "I thought that you'd be boring and that you'd be an anchor. That's not how I feel about you now. I know for a fact that we'll work well together."

"I can't do that. I can't have you to choose me and have me running back and forth between seeing after my mama, dealing with work and school… and then after we're married, there would be no time for us if we decide to have kids."

"I want 'em. I want a lot of them. A big house filled with kids and us and your mama will be there too… just give this a chance."

"I can't. If you knock me off my path, then I'll never be sure of myself. This was all a competition, and I don't want to compete with someone else. I can't risk the chance of getting hurt. I have a lot to focus on. So let's just enjoy our last two and a half days together and say our goodbyes like adults. We said we'd be friends afterward, right?"

"I don't accept that," he said sternly as he squeezed her hands. "I'm not hurting you at all, and I can see us together for the long haul. This chick that I have to see means nothing to me. I want you. Fuck the contract. Fuck the money. I've earned what I have, and I'm trying to earn you. You're like a jigsaw puzzle that I'm piecing together, and even though you confuse me most of the time, I'm still trying. Don't turn me down."

"Diego—"

"Christina, say yes and close your trap," Regina said through a raspy voice. "Some of us are trying to recover over here. You always got to be hard."

Diego dropped his head and tucked his lips between his teeth to hold in his laugh.

"Mama, go to sleep," she giggled. "I'm trying to let him down gently."

"Well, you wouldn't need to if you just stop thinking about everything else. I'm here; I'm alive, and I'm fine. Now go and fall in love for Christ's sake and be done with it. I'm going back to sleep."

"So what's up, Chris?" Diego asked her. "You got two votes that say you should go ahead and do this."

"Fine," she grunted. "But you still have to spend your week with the other woman. If we're going to do this, then we need to do it right. I don't need you to regret me later on down the line."

"I won't. And I'll spend my week with her, but I'm not gonna like it."

She smacked her lips. "Come on, Diego. Cooperate."

"Fine," he laughed. "Just promise me that you'll be here when I get back."

"I will."

He grabbed her jaws and laid a kiss on her lips, forgetting where he was at the moment.

—

The vibrating phone in Diego's pocket woke him from a sound sleep. He lifted his head out of Christina's lap on the couch and wiped the corners of his mouth with the back of his hand. By the time he fetched his phone, the call had stopped. He gently pulled Christina down onto the couch and straightened her pillows underneath her head to make her more comfortable and planted a kiss on her cheek. With his eyes still on her, he backed out of the room and into the hall where he returned Silk's phone call.

"For real, for real… you need to come see me," Silk said urgently on the other end. "I ain't had enough shit for myself all day. Come holla at your boy. ASAP."

Diego hung up and leaned his head against the wall. He didn't know how much more he was going to be able to take when dealing with his work schedule and not being able to see enough of Christina. All that he could hope for was that the next week would go by as quickly as possible.

His phone vibrated again but this time, it had been Chandler. He narrowed his eyes at the screen and wondered why he could've been calling him. Instead of sending it to voicemail, he answered. "What it is?"

"When you get some time, come and scoop me," Chandler said miserably. "Man, I got to get out of this house. I feel like the walls are closing in on me. Angel's acting funny and shit, and I don't have shit to do."

"Be there in a minute. I got some business to take care of."

"Cool. I'll be standing out front."

Diego hung up and finally noticed the time. It seemed as if he and Christina slept the day away with it being close to 8PM. By the time he made it to Chandler's apartment, it was a little after.

Chandler had gotten into the SUV and slammed the door, then almost immediately buckled his seatbelt. "Man, you can't have a motherfucker addicted to the night life and then turn over a new leaf in the blink of an eye," he complained. "I think I have insomnia now. I've been writing short stories and scripts and shit to make myself fall asleep but it ain't workin'. What's wrong with you?"

"I'm sorry," Diego lightly chuckled as he pulled away from the apartment complex. "Trying to keep up with Christina and this business ain't easy. I bit off more than I can chew but I'm handling this shit the best I can."

"I feel you. But what's up with Angel?"

"Nigga, I don't know. Honestly, I think that he's a little uptight 'cause he thinks I offended him. Roll me up, Chan."

"You must've known I had my shit with me," he grinned. Chandler reached into the backseat for his backpack and dug out what all he needed to roll a blunt so that the both of them could rid themselves of their troubles.

On his dash, Diego's phone rang. He retrieved it and saw that it was Dena calling. Tonight, he decided not to send her to voicemail. He wanted to be a man and face her for a change. "You know that I'm not supposed to be talkin' to you, right?" he asked her. "You've been calling me all week while I'm spending time with someone else. That doesn't seem at all disrespectful to you? How would you feel if she blew me up while we were trying to spend time?"

"I just wanted to hear from you, that's all," she giggled. "I really enjoyed our time together, and I figured I could check up on you and remind you that I'm interested and that I can't wait for our week to begin. I have a lot planned for us. A friend of mine is performing at a strip club downtown, and I thought maybe we could go and blow stacks on her. You know, stunt on some niggas and unwind while doing so."

"Sounds like a plan, but I'm gonna have to hit you on Sunday morning when my week officially ends with her."

"I like how you're handling this when you know that we've enjoyed ourselves so much that I know I'm number one."

"You think so, huh?"

"I know so, baby. I'm a grown woman about mine, so ain't no hard feelings because you're getting your dick wet right now. When mama comes home, you know what it'll be. Have your fun now but all of that shit stops when I arrive. I'll see you Sunday."

"Yea." He hung up and had to laugh at her for trying to show out when she didn't know the situation. Of course he enjoyed his date with Dena, but he'd grown into a completely different man since then. Dena had her work cut out for her if she thought that she was better than Christina.

Chandler passed Diego the blunt and said, "I already had a couple of fingers rolled up. You don't know how much getting out of the house means to me right now. Nigga, all I want to do is blow and sleep."

"You ain't the only one."

"Can I stay with y'all for a couple of days? I need to be as far away from the house as possible. My mama is driving me up the wall, bro."

"That shouldn't be a problem. Christina's a bitch sometimes, but she likes to take care of people. She wouldn't mind."

"Oh, so you got you a Mother Teresa type of bitch?"

"Watch your mouth," Diego sternly warned him and pulled from his blunt. "We got to make some moves right fast, so keep your mouth shut and don't make eye contact."

Chandler fondly nodded and took out his phone to peruse through his social media accounts.

Shortly after Diego made his first stop, his phone rang on the dash. Chandler grabbed it and saw Christina's name on the screen. A smile spread across his face, and he took the liberty of answering on his friend's behalf. "What it is, shawty, what it do?"

"That was lame as hell," she tiredly said. "Who is this?"

"Chandler, but you can call me Chan. What's up, Christina? I've heard a lot about you."

"Oh? I've heard nothing of you, sadly. No disrespect intended. I just need to ask Diego more questions. Where is he?"

"Handling business. You want to leave him a message?"

"Actually, yes. Tell him that my mama is putting me out of her room and I need him to come and get me when he's done. I'm tired and I'm hungry."

Chandler opened his mouth to say something, but Diego came jogging to the car with a backpack strapped onto his back. "Hold on. You can tell him. Gimme a minute."

"What?" Diego asked after he tossed his bag into the backseat.

"Your girl is on the phone. She said to get your motherfuckin' ass to her because she's hungry and sleepy, and she's gonna stomp the shit out of you because she knows that you're out here fuckin' with them other hoes."

Diego smirked and snatched his iPhone out of Chandler's hand and pressed it against his ear. "Hey, baby," he greeted her. "What do you want to eat?"

Christina could hear him slam the backdoor and shrugged as if he could see her.

"Babe? What you want? If I pick something random then you're gonna be mad."

"I don't know," she whined.

He sat in the driver's seat and had to pull his phone away from his ear and look at it to make sure it was really her on the other end. "Hold on, who is this? My Chrissy doesn't whine with her *mean* ass."

"I'm not mean," she sang as she stomped her foot for emphasis. "I'm serious, Diego. I hadn't eaten anything since the day before, and I barely ate then. On top of that, I'm sleepy. Please hurry."

"I'm coming," he chuckled. "Hang tight and I'll be right there."

Chandler burst into laughter after his friend hung up and threw his phone onto his dash.

"Fuck so funny?"

"Nigga… you have a girlfriend."

"So?"

"Never thought I'd see the day. You got a leash around your neck."

"I'd rather have one than not to have one at all, lame ass nigga. And don't answer my phone again. I don't want you fuckin' up my business. Google some twenty-four spots or see what time some barbecue places close. My babe loves soul food."

"Your babe?" Chandler asked skeptically. When Diego looked over at him, Chandler's expression was as if Diego had slapped him in the face.

"Yea, nigga, my *babe*!"

"This nigga's all in love and shit!"

"I ain't said all of that. I said she was my babe. That means she belongs to me and nobody else, and I'm off the market… even though I made her a promise that I'd still spend my week with that other bitch."

Chandler slowly shook his head. "Pass all the pussy you don't want over here to me. I ain't passin' it up; you can believe that."

Diego's phone rang again, and he rolled his eyes at it just as he stopped his SUV at a stoplight. "I swear to God this job ain't a nine to five, my nigga," he complained. Then he picked up his phone and verified that the ringtone and contact ID was his father. "What's up, pop? You good? I tried to call you earlier."

"Silk said that we're having territorial problems with vermin. Apparently they're all over the house," he slurred.

Diego frowned at how he sounded. Obviously, Ramone woke up just to chug more liquor and Lean. It would take some time for him to get over the betrayal. Time that, to Diego, they didn't have.

"I'm about to send a kite to the other line for some Haitians. They're good underpaid exterminators. Let me know what the bill is and get on top of that."

Diego bit his bottom lip while listening to his father. He reckoned that Ramone wouldn't know what the hell he'd said when the conversation was over.

Ramone hung up the phone and left his son to do his job. Though he was growing weary of it, he prayed that he'd adjust well enough because it seemed as though he started off as nothing but a trainee but was promoted to CEO within the blink of an eye. His nostrils flared as he tossed his phone back up on the dash and sucked up his personal issues to get the job done.

# Chapter 10

Diego opened the front door of his condo for Christina and carried her luggage inside for her. She didn't care for him being a gentleman at the moment; she wanted her baked potato that had been fully loaded with chopped beef, sour cream and a mountain of cheddar cheese. Diego had gotten her a side of ribs and macaroni and cheese to go with her potato salad. Chandler didn't know if he was trailing behind her for her food or her backside, but either one of them could have had a bite taken out of it.

"Chan! Living room!" Diego warned him from his bedroom. "Sit your little puppy in heat ass down somewhere. If she elbows the fuck out of you, I'm not gonna be held responsible."

"I just want some of her ribs," he happily said as he plopped down on the leather sofa. "I mean, Christina, you're fine and all… but a nigga just want a rib."

"Why didn't you order that shit when we were there then?"

"Nigga, 'cause you ain't offered!"

Diego squeezed his temple and reentered to stand behind Christina and softly place his hand on her hips while she sat on the high chair at his dining room table. He placed his lips gently at her ear and kissed it. "Do you feel like sharing with that hungry ass nigga, baby?"

"He can have some," she shyly giggled. "You didn't have to try and sweet talk me just to get him some of my ribs."

"Oh, that wasn't sweet talking you." He pat her hip and snagged a rib out of her to-go container and handed it off to his begging friend. "Next time, speak the fuck up or else stay hungry."

"Mmm, Diego!" Christina called him with a full mouth. She then licked her fingers and swallowed the contents before she could continue. "My wallet is in my luggage. How much did you pay for—"

"I ain't even hearin' you right now, shawty." He waved her off and had gone back into his room to shower and change clothes.

Christina finished off her food and showed Chandler how to turn on the living room Smart TV with a wave of his hand. She was quite surprised that he hadn't known how to do so but figured that they really hadn't spent much time in the house or paying attention to the TV when they were at Diego's place. Then she traveled into the master bathroom and pulled apart the glass doors that housed the young prince and his steam.

Diego turned to her with his body lathered and glistening, and cocked a smile at her. "What? You want to join me or something?"

"Maybe," she smirked. "You owe me, remember?"

"How could I forget?"

With his teeth gripping his bottom lip, he helped Christina to remove her top and waited impatiently for her to shimmy out of her denim short shorts and laced panties and socks. Then he pulled her inside of his shower and fused their lips together. Finally, Christina surrendered and submitted to whatever Diego had waiting for her. She didn't have to fight with him; she just let herself go in the moment and offered up herself for whatever he had in return.

What she hadn't told him was of the good scolding that Regina had given her before she kicked her out of the hospital. She reminded her daughter that you only live once and that certain opportunities will never present themselves again. While indulging in their tongues tangoing, she could feel Diego's palms on the back of her thighs as he lifted her so that she could rest her back on the spa bench, and he wrapped her ankles around his neck. Though she stuck her hand up to his lower abdomen to keep him from driving inside of her too deeply, it hadn't stopped him. He rammed into her and loved it. Diego couldn't stop himself. He didn't want to have any more control, so he threw it out and gave her all of what he had.

Chandler sat out on the couch and was sending out random text messages, one of them including how stupid Angel was for being so easily offended. Afterward, he sent his friend another message to remind him that they were all cool, so nothing like Diego trying to come into his own should've offended him in any type of way. He said that no matter what, they were supposed to be there to support him besides taking things personally. Angel figured it'd be best for him to see his friend face to face instead of sitting at home a few units away and text back and forth like women. The sight he stumbled upon was one that made his blood simmer. Christina's hands and breasts were pressed against the shower doors, and it had almost given him a hard on until Diego's hand mashed against hers. Angel's lids fluttered while he tried his damnedest to keep himself from screaming out how dirty Diego was for taking advantage of such an innocent girl like her.

"Harder," Christina shrieked.

"You sure?" Diego huffed.

"Please? Don't hold anything away from me. Give me what you got."

Angel was sick to his stomach. He stormed out of the condo and hadn't even said a word to Chandler about it all.

To switch positions, Diego sat on the spa bench and made Christina mount him. The girl wasn't an expert. She had only one sexual partner that lasted no more than 5 minutes, but for Diego, she made it work. He squeezed her cheeks and made her rock with his penetration. With his head inside of her bosom, Christina wrapped her arms around his neck and tried not to squeeze him too hard. Her orgasm was strongly approaching and she needed it, just to feel something else with Diego besides the weight of her heart. When she felt that tingle grow from within her core and consume her, she sucked in a long breath just as Diego shuttered underneath her chin. He'd pulled out of her and released his semen somewhere in the rushing hot waters. One last gentle kiss he delivered to her chest plate and leaned his head back to look up at her. Christina held his face within her hands, but she feared their escapade was far from over.

—

Almost two hours later and four orgasms after the first, the tired pair retired to Diego's king sized canopy bed inside of the master's suite. He lay on his back in nothing but his Calvin Klein briefs with Christina's wild curls relaxing against his bicep. She lay on her side, dressed in a white dress shirt that belonged to him, with her left leg over his midsection, and she stroked the C that was tattooed on his peck.

"Why do they call you Dutch?" she quietly asked him, remembering Chandler refer to him as such when they were in the car. "Is it because your father is 'the Duke'?"

"Partly," he tiredly mumbled as he stroked her arm. "His middle name is actually Duke, and because of it he gave me the middle name Dutch."

"Really? So you just willingly let people call you by your middle name?"

"Pretty much. What's your middle name?"

"I'm not telling you that."

"You might as well. You know what mine is."

"Rae," she huffed. "Christina Rae Jackson."

"I would laugh at you, but I'm too tired."

"What are you going to do when all of this over?"

"Go to college," he readily answered. "I mean, the fast life is the life for some, but it's not for me. I figured out so much about my dad because of what he does for a living, and I don't want to be like that. The money is good and all but these long nights and early days ain't gonna last long for me. I look at it as being an intern or an apprentice. It's a stepping stone for the bigger game. With this business and how well I'm workin' it, I'll be at the top of somebody's fortune five hundred company in no time. What about you?"

"After graduation, I'm going to work the circuit for a little bit and open my own accounting firm somewhere. And then comes marriage and love in eleven years."

He turned his face and stared into hers with pressing brows until she opened her eyes and found him there. "Eleven years, Christina? Really?"

"Eleven. Diego, I don't want to argue. You asked me and I told you. I didn't plan on marrying you as the contract stated as soon as you chose me, but I guess that's something that's going to have to change. Yes, I'll marry you if you ask. Unfortunately, the kids won't come until I'm financially ready for them."

"I can have us financially ready, babe."

"It's only been a few days. You don't think you're rushing this?"

"No. *Fuck* no. I know who I want and what I want, and that includes a house full of babies and a real damn family. That means your mama's coming with us. Christina, I won't take your independence away from you, I just need you to know what I want.

I'm laying it all out on the table for you. You can take it or leave it. I'd prefer if you took it, though."

"Can we just enjoy our last day together, please?"

"Then let's live like it's our last." Diego climbed on top of her and pulled her legs around his waist, to make sure he sexed them both to sleep.

# Chapter 11

Diego decided only to make one run on Friday afternoon, and it was to pick up the work from the projects and take them to Silk and left it up to him to do the books. He had other things to do like plan out his evening with Christina. He'd taken her to see her mother and they had lunch with her, shared a laugh or two and stayed until she'd fallen asleep. Then he took her— along with Chandler and a young lady that he'd known since high school by the name of Rachel— out shopping. Since Christina was a little tightwad who didn't like handouts, she'd playfully banter back and forth with Diego to keep his pricey gifts to himself.

Still, he paid for dinner out at a bistro downtown. The foursome enjoyed Rachel's company and promised to see more of her. It left Christina to wonder how come Rachel hadn't had relations with Diego after openly admitting that she didn't know why women went so crazy over him. Christina took a page out Diego's book and assumed that Rachel was a lesbian. They all settled down on the hill behind the condos after the skies were left navy blue. Christina was sitting between Diego's legs and had sensual kisses planted on her cheeks every time she looked over her shoulder at him, but would lean back to relax whenever he wasn't being an asshole about something he said.

Chandler tried his hardest to flex his smooth verbal skills on Rachel, but the 5'5" chocolate diva would put her hand in his face and say "Next subject." He went in again for a line before his phone sang Angel's ringtone.

"Yea?" he answered.

"Man, have that nigga come and get what his daddy dropped on him. I keep knockin' on the door, but nobody's answering their phones."

"Their bad," Chandler laughed. "Chrissy and Dutch's phones are on the chargers upstairs."

"Whatever man."

"Dutch!" Chandler called him after he hung up. "Angel's got something from Duke."

Diego nodded but took his attention back to Christina. He wrapped his arms around her and sealed their lips to feel her tongue against his yet again.

Rachel flipped her long locks over her shoulder and said, "Y'all are just too cute. Dutch, you're really into her, aren't you? I've never seen you like this. Honestly, I don't think I like staring at motherfuckers kissing. Come here, Chandler. Tongue me down, daddy."

He shrugged and leaned over, but she mushed his face jokingly to keep him away.

Christina took Diego's Miami Heat snapback off his head and hid their faces behind it just so that Rachel wouldn't have to watch.

"Dutch!" Angel called him from the breezeway of the unit. He had a duffle strapped across his torso that wrinkled his white t-shirt. "Come and get your shit, bro!"

Diego softly took away his hat from Christina's fingers and sat it atop his head backward, then pecked her lips one last time before he got up to take the duffle from his friend. "What's up?" he asked him as he brushed his denim shorts off. "What you sound so fuckin' mad about now?"

"I ain't your errand boy," he angrily told him as he lifted the strap from his shoulder and dropped the bag at Diego's feet.

"Fuck is your problem, A? It got to be something deeper than you thinking that a nigga offended you. Which one of your bitches did I fuck? Which one of 'em got your chest all swole up and shit?"

Angel massaged his goatee and took a sloppy step away from Diego so that he could contain his anger. "Which one of my *bitches*?"

"Which one of your bitches, nigga?"

"Christina. That's who."

Without even thinking, Diego reached back to three weeks ago and slammed his fist into the side of Angel's baby face.

Hearing the sound of smacking skin, the others turned around to see what the hell had happened. Chandler had gotten up and run over to his boys to keep them from throwing blows, but with how hard Diego hit Angel, he wasn't going to be able to fight back if he tried. He knocked a part of the boy's motor skills loose.

Chandler grabbed Diego arms from behind and backed him away from Angel so that he could pick himself— along with his life, soul, and brain matter— off of the concrete. "Chill," Chandler warned him. "What the fuck is this bad blood between y'all?"

"This nigga got a motherfuckin' problem, but he wants to bring my girl into the mix like I'm some type of bitch ass nigga?" Diego complained with a grimace.

"She ain't nothin' to you but a toy," Angel grumbled as he waddled toward a steal stairway a few inches away from where he gathered himself. "She's a fuckin' pawn in your games."

"You don't know what the fuck you're talkin' about! Have you been snortin'?"

"I don't need powder to see that you're a fuck up. I hope you enjoyed fuckin' her, 'cause she'll know pretty soon how much of a fucked up person you are."

"What's he talking about?" Christina asked as she and Rachel appeared from the side of Diego and Chandler.

"Go back down the hill," Diego instructed them both. "This nigga's out of his fuckin' mind. Are you jealous, A?"

"Jealous of what?" He wickedly laughed while wiping blood away from his top lip. Angel did a damn good job at concealing the pain of his broken nose. "Stay, Christina. You're a good girl. You should know how you should stay the fuck away from him. When he gets his money, he's just gonna leave you for a big booty bitch that ain't got shit else better to do besides blow him and walk away like a confused, abandoned puppy."

Diego flinched when trying to get away from Chandler, but Rachel stood in front of him to try and get him to calm down.

"I think that maybe you should give him some space and then come and try to talk to him at another time," Christina reasoned.

"He doesn't care about anyone or anything besides him and his money. You see I'm the nigga's best friend, and I'm close to washing his draws once he sits on his new throne."

"Okay, you should really leave before he gets away from Chandler."

"He didn't remember shit about you on your first date. That was me who took the time out to keep your info in my notes."

"Good for you… but you should really just leave."

"Ask him how many babies he killed this week."

"What?" Christina's neck popped back.

"He didn't tell you that either? How he had to make a payout for silence? Well, that's only because he doesn't want to share his fortunes with anyone. Not even his own ki—"

Successfully, Diego tore away from Chandler's grip and pushed Rachel out of the way to finish Angel off. Christina kept trying to get him off of Angel, but it was no use. Instead of trying to tear them apart, she stomped up the stairs and took the journey to the front of the unit so that she could go inside of the condo and gather her things. Rachel was right behind her.

"Christina," she called from the front door, only stopping to slip out of her Chanel sandals before jogging around the massive apartment to find the young woman who had her world shaken by what had been said.

Christina was enraged. She pulled everything that she could get her hands on out of the drawers in the spare room and stuffed them inside of her luggage that she placed on the bed.

"Christina, please listen," Rachel said softly from the doorway. "You don't understand."

"Well help me!" she lashed, whirling her head around to see the shapely young woman standing there in her denim jumper. "Help me understand why it was that he couldn't put you in the pool and make you his wife for the money!"

"Because I'm a lesbian!" Rachel shouted.

Christina's jaw dropped and her eyes bulged. What she assumed was correct.

"You don't understand the fact that I was just like them. Privileged and spoiled as hell. No, my daddy didn't need to trap me in a contract. On my seventeenth birthday, a few weeks before I started my senior year of high school, he told me that I had to choose a school. College was the furthest thing from my mind when I was only out looking to get ate out by a sexy dime piece who thought that I could save her from her troubles. I had to get my shit together, just like he's doing now. I was just lucky enough to have a whole year to do so. Unlike Dutch, my daddy told me that it was either college or find a bridge to sleep under after graduation. Don't you see? Me and my boys were all the same with how we didn't give a fuck about anything besides parties, money, bitches and weed. I see the way Dutch looks at you, and it's not the same as how he looked at all of those other girls. He knew that I was coming home before my college graduation and begged me to come and check you out. I texted him under the table at dinner and told him that I liked you and that I thought you could balance his wild ass out. But you're just gonna leave him? I don't know what the fuck Angel's problem is, but he got what was coming to him for jumping stupid. You can't go. I'm asking you as someone who has seen his dirt firsthand. Stay?"

Christina closed her mouth and tightened her jaw. "I knew this was all bullshit."

"Please, Chrissy. Stay for him! Angel's just on some dumb shit right now!"

"You want to do something for me?" she yelled at Rachel. "Use your nice luxury car to take me home. That's what you can do."

"Chris. Come on."

"Take me home or get the fuck out of my way when I walk out of that door!"

The girls locked eyes for what seemed like forever and Rachel crumbled on the inside for her friend. Even though her graduation was on Wednesday, she'd have to come right back to Jackson to make sure he wouldn't do something stupid like stalk Christina in order to get her attention.

"Whatever," she mumbled and helped Christina pack the last of her things.

---

Diego flexed his fist while Chandler helped Angel back to his unit. Diego shook his head and picked up the duffle to go up the stairs but changed paths in direction when seeing Christina and Rachel round the back of Rachel's Range Rover.

"What the fuck?" he mumbled with his face contorted. "Chrissy!" he shouted.

She hadn't looked at him before she slammed the door. Rachel pushed the start button on her ignition and backed out of her parking space.

Holding his breath, Diego took a running start for the moving SUV. “Don’t do this!” he cried. Finally, he’d caught up to the car when Rachel shifted gears to leave the complex. He banged on the passenger side window to get Christina’s attention, but she wasn’t looking at him. “Baby! Stay! Don’t leave! I can explain it all! I did this for *us*!”

Rachel picked up speed, though she didn’t want to, and left her friend running behind her SUV like a crazed man.

Christina chewed on the inside of her jaw as her eyes clouded. She didn’t want to leave him, but she couldn’t believe she actually had given her all to him instead of going back on her plans to keep it as all a game that she was sure that she wasn’t going to win. She opened up to him, and he had secrets. If he could have secrets, to Christina, she wondered what else he was keeping away. She wanted to beat herself for allowing him to speak those sweet nothings into her ear, but there was nothing she could do about it other than pick herself back up and try to continue with what she had going before her mother even entered her into a competition in the first place.

# Chapter 12

If things couldn't get any worse for Prince Diego, he'd tried numerous times to get through to Christina without it being successful. He'd gone as far as to repeatedly checking his Tumblr page to see if she'd reblogged anything and only found one poster that was a lengthy complaint about finals approaching. It did, however, make him remember that she was taking her finals on Wednesday and Thursday, but he couldn't wait that long to see her.

He tried to work and consumed his thoughts with it so that he would try to forget about her, but it didn't work. Dena had arrived only two days prior, and he used his work as an excuse to stay away from her. Constantly he'd call and text in hopes that Christina would answer, but she wouldn't. He didn't know what her work and school schedule was, so he'd try to sit out on the porch until someone called about money. He figured that she'd be at the hospital with Regina if she didn't come home, but when he'd get there, he would always miss her. Today he wasn't taking any of that shit from her. She was going to sit there and hear him out.

He counted up early and set aside stacks for his father and some for himself, and ventured down to Christina's apartment with Chandler in tow. He told his friend to wait at the car while he got his girl back, and obediently, that's precisely what Chandler did in hopes that whatever dark cloud that was hanging over Diego's head would float off already.

Diego knocked four times on the backdoor and flexed his jaw. He knew that she had to be home this time. Someone sent him a text that said that they saw her get off the city bus. "Open the fuckin' door before I kick it in, Christina!" he angrily warned her.

Christina swung the door open and tightened her lips at Diego. Just as she went to shut the door back, he caught it and forced it open.

"Fuck wrong with you?" he shouted at her as he stepped inside. "You don't want to answer no calls? You don't want to return a nigga's texts and shit?"

"Whatever," she mumbled.

He slammed the back door and grabbed her wrist, but Christina yanked away and pushed him. "Put your hands on me again, Chrissy! I motherfuckin' dare you!"

"Fuck you, Diego!" she screamed. "You can't come in here and start yelling and expect me to hop to! I don't need you, your support or your bullshit voicemails that you've been leaving me!"

"*Bullshit*?"

"Yea, bullshit! I'm not these other bitches that'll take your sappy ass 'I'm sorry' pleas and hop on the dick when I see you! You can't boss up and expect me to shut the fuck up. I'm not them, my nigga!"

He reached out and grabbed her jaws within his hand and stepped closer. His face was hard, and Christina hadn't scared him a bit. Her attitude was only going to get her into a situation that she couldn't get herself out of. "Who the fuck are you talkin' to?" he gritted. "Who the fuck do you think you're talkin' to?"

She shoved his hand away and took two hard steps closer to leave no space between them. "I'm talking to *you*," she hissed. "You're a crybaby ass little boy who can't leave well enough a-damn-lone. I'm out of this competition, and I'm out of whatever game it is that you're trying to play just to get your money from your daddy."

"I ain't played no games with you, and I've worked for every-fucking-thing I got from that nigga. I busted my ass to get every last dime, and even you can't tell me no different."

"Oh, you ain't played, huh? How many babies *did* you kill, Diego? You never answered the question."

"I was trying to tell your simple ass that I did it because I was trying to protect what we had. At least I thought we were getting somewhere, and I actually started to like your mean ass. I didn't want to be bothered with baby mamas or have you to try and compete with the attention of kids that *we* didn't have. But you stepped the fuck off on a nigga. It's nice to see that all of this was really a game to you. Like everything we shared was nothing to you."

"Be real, my nigga. It was nothing to *you*. All you were doing was playing a fucking part to get your money, and you didn't want those kids in the way of doing that because you're selfish."

"Tread real lightly, lil' mama. You're gonna fuck around and say some shit that's either gonna get you fucked up or you're gonna end up lookin' stupid as fuck."

"Whatever, Diego. Get the fuck out of my house and out of my face. My week with you is up, and now you can choose the next bitch so you can get your money and go back to the life you were living before you got *trapped*."

"Tell me something..." He wiped his mouth and backed toward the door before he could finish his statement. "How long were *you* pretending with me? Hmm? How long did you plan on putting on an act for me? This is the same bitch I saw at the restaurant when we first met. I knew that bitch was going to show her face. It ain't the fact that you didn't have a life before me, it was the fact that you couldn't get one because you were such a fuckin' bitch with her head so far up her own ass that the only thing she knew in life was shit. Fuck you, Christina. I regret ever fallin' for your stupid ass." And with that, he opened the back door, threw her the bird and slammed it as hard as he could.

Chandler got off the hood of the Escalade when he saw his friend angrily marching down the walkway and assumed the worst. The day wasn't supposed to play out like it did and even everyone around them knew that they were supposed to stay together. If only Angel hadn't thrown that monkey wrench in the plans. Diego had something for that.

---

The SUV came to a slow stop at the condos, but it hadn't been in front of Diego's unit. Chandler fumbled with his seatbelt before he could muster the courage to ask a question or two.

"W-w-w-what are we doing here?" he stuttered. He noticed Diego's low brow and the way he was hunched over the steering wheel, even after he had taken his keys out of the ignition. There was something dark about him, and it didn't sit right with Chandler. "Look, you have a bad ass bitch at your crib. You should go there and wear her back out. Don't do nothin' crazy."

"Shut the fuck up!" Diego roared and drew a .50 caliber pistol from underneath his seat.

"D!" Chandler shouted as he threw his hands up. Fear flooded his dark brown and fat face. "Come on, man! Think about this shit! Just go home, bro!"

"Fuck that." Diego threw the door to his SUV open while Chandler grabbed his phone from out of his back pocket to phone Ramone. Diego jogged up the steps and knocked on the first door on his left and waited for somebody to answer.

Chandler paced in front of the Cadillac, hoping and praying that Ramone would answer already before his son had done something that he was going to regret.

"This better be good," Ramone stated after the fourth ring. "What do you want, boy?"

"Duke! It's Dutch!" Chandler panicked. "We're at Angel's! He has a gun!"

"Who has a gun?"

"Dutch! We went to Christina's and then we came here! I don't know if he's gonna kill him or threaten him!"

"Don't move. I'm on my way."

Diego pushed past the girl who had opened the front door and jogged up the stairs inside of the of the condo, threw Angel's bedroom door open and pulled him out the closet that had been the makeshift booth for his home studio. Diego gave no fucks about the other three guys there to record a mixtape that would probably receive no downloads. He dragged Angel to the middle of his master suite and pistol whipped him.

"Motherfucker!" he shouted. He'd blacked out. "You've been my nigga for years! You want to stab me in my motherfuckin' back? You want to be jealous of everything I have and fuck shit up for me?"

"Diego!" Chandler screamed from the doorway.

He stopped swinging and stood tall, pointing his gun directly at his second oldest friend. "Back the fuck up, Chan," he ordered as his chest heaved.

"We're boys," Chandler tried to reason. This was the bravest thing he'd ever done. "I know he fucked up, but you can't kill him. It'll be on your conscience for the rest of your life. Think about it for a moment."

Diego snapped the top of his gun and it made the other three in the room duck for cover and hide behind whatever piece of furniture that would shield them from a ricocheted bullet.

Chandler slowly raised his hands and his rising and falling chest stopped. He'd sucked up all of his pride and took a slow step toward his friend. "Listen to me," he said lowly. "This is not what you want to do. You're already getting your life together. That in itself shows Christina that you're worthy, no matter what mistakes you already made. At least, right now, you can give her some time to think about everything and then finesse her. You know you're good at that sort of thing."

"Shut the fuck up! You don't know what you're talkin' about!"

"It's okay, D. You don't see it right now, but you know that what I'm saying is true." Chandler stepped over Angel's squirming body and stopped, just shy of an inch of the nose of his friend's gun. "I know you love her. I can see it. You've done things for her that you would never do."

"Move the fuck out of the way," Diego warned him between closed teeth.

"I know how it hurts. I know. Look who you're talking to. You know I know how bad it feels when another nigga steps in the way of me trying to get the girl I crave for. How many times have I had my heart broken? Huh? How many times have you told me to man the fuck up and go find a bitch who'll bust it open for the moment?"

"I'm not tellin' you again, Chan."

"Well, I'm telling you to man the fuck up and wait patiently for your woman. Killing him is only going to put you in prison, and then she'll never want you. Diego, I'd rather you take me than him."

"Get... the fuck... outta the way."

"I can't do that. I can't let you fuck up everything that you're trying to do right now."

"Fuck the problem is?" another voice asked. A man snapped the top of his .9 millimeter and aimed it at Diego. One of the young men who dove behind Angel's bed had pulled his phone from his pocket and sent a text to a friend who was waiting for them in the car.

Diego felt that he didn't have anything to live for so he pointed his piece at the mystery man in the doorway. "It's either you or this bleedin' motherfucker on the floor," he said. "Back the fuck off, nigga. This bullet wasn't meant for you."

"Come on," Chandler spoke up. "You were going to shoot me, not him. Focus, Diego, for once in your life."

"I guess we gon' be some shot up motherfuckers then," the man in the doorway said. "My homie is in here somewhere, and a nigga with a grudge is holding him hostage. I ain't leaving until I leave with my niggas."

The click of a gun sounded and Diego and Chandler looked over at the door, with Diego's gun waving back to the man there. A dark figure stood behind the man, and a voice warned, "You point a gun at my boy then you're pointin' one at me too. Put your little toy pistol away and walk the fuck off. Your boys are at the wrong place and at the wrong damn time. Beat feet, nigga."

"You called my old man?" Diego shouted at Chandler. "You stalled me out?"

"You weren't going to listen to me!" he yelled back. "You think I want to lose my only two friends over a girl that you can get back, over some bullshit?"

"Fuck you, Chan!"

"No, nigga, fuck *you*! You're sittin' over here cryin' over Christina and about to kill your boy because he was a pussy about his feelings and shit! He was wrong, and now you're wrong! Call that shit even and keep it moving!"

Diego's finger squeezed his trigger but the sound of a different gun went off, and Diego felt a burn on his skin across his wrist. His head whirled around to the doorway with a shocked expression on his face.

Ramone grabbed the back of the man's shirt who had been too frightened to move with a gun pressing into the back of his skull and moved him out of the way. "I didn't want to shoot you, so I grazed you," he told his son. "Drop the goddamn gun and let's go."

"I don't need you to fight my battles," Diego gritted.

"I ain't fightin' a damn battle; I'm saving my son from being stupid." Ramone reloaded the chamber by pulled the latch on his gun back and pointed it at his son's chest. "You want to throw your life away over a pussy, then I'll take it before I have to pay a visit to you in them cages. You got three seconds."

Diego narrowed his eyes while Chandler's had gone dancing back and forth between the duo and his heart pounded. He could easily wined up injured or killed, no matter who decided to pull the trigger.

"Three..." Ramone counted off. "Two..."

Diego tightened his jaw with his hard and blackened eyes on his ex-friend. He wanted to pull the trigger so badly that it almost had given him an erection. He had a life changing decision to make because he knew that his father would've shot him because he had already given it a second thought, and Ramone always kept his promises. Should he kill his old friend and end up losing his life? Or should he surrender and continue on the path that he was already on when rebuilding his life? It was far beyond Christina at this point. It was about life and death.

*"One..."*

Diego declined his arm and pushed Chandler out of the way to take his heavy foot to Angel's ribs. Then he spat on him and tore away from the room.

# Chapter 13

Dena paced impatiently on the hardwood floors of the living room. Besides the sound of the tall black grandfather clock in the corner that had been ticking the time away, you could hear her heels clacking and her unsteady breaths. She was trying her best to keep herself composed when thinking that maybe Diego wasn't into her the way he was when they shared their first date. Maybe he just didn't see her the same after his week with the other woman. Usually, the 20-year-old was very confident, with the curve and sway of her round hips to her plump and luscious lips. She made sure to keep herself up; whether it be by having her hair infused with extensions or having to workout at the gym while using a waist shaper to make sure her waist was tiny and corseted. Dena was sure that she could make Diego see that she was the one, with her high-class style and her sense of humor, her dimples and her large double D breasts. She was every man's wet dream. The girl was built like Jessica Rabbit for crying out loud. Any man to reject the caramel skin tone woman was a damn fool.

A knock came at the front door, and without thinking she rushed to it in her 6-inch pumps and answered it. The person on the other side was not who she had been expecting. A woman stepped in as if she owned the condo, just about an inch shorter than Dena in a pair of Giuseppe heels that made her mouth water. Little did she know, by her eyes being glued to the woman's shoes, she had given her confirmation that she was a part of her "tribe", if you will. Red leather wing sandals with a Zanotti design featuring an open toe, multiple ankle straps with side fastenings, a branded insole and stiletto high heels strutted through the living room. Dena's eyes caught on to the woman's black short suit with a matching jacket that stopped at a quarter length that she had identified to be a designer from Chanel. The woman's entire outfit, including her weave, had to be priced at no more than $14,000. The estimate came about when the taut and fit woman took a seat on Diego's white couch and sat her red leather Hermes vintage bag beside her then pulled a pack of cigarettes out of it, along with a lighter.

"Can I help you?" Dena asked nervously. "If you're looking for Diego, he's not here."

"I know," Markiesha said sordidly as she eyed the young woman with disgust dripping from her face. She then held up her cigarette and lit it, and Dena figured that she had to have gone to one of the best finishing schools to puff her cigarette without disturbing the red lipstick and gloss she wore. Markiesha sat back on the couch and crossed her legs, blew her smoke and whipped her side bang away from her right eye. "Allow me to properly introduce myself. My name is Markiesha *Caraway*. I would've used my key, but knowing my *son,* he's probably gone and changed the locks on me."

"Well, he's not—"

"I know he's not. I came for you." Markiesha took another slow pull from her cigarette while Dena stood in front of her looking as confused as ever. "You're just a baby version of me," she said honestly. Smoke seeped from her nostrils, and it should've been Dena's cue to decline any offer considering that the woman sat here looking like the sexy devil reincarnate. "I know what you want from my son, and honestly, I don't blame you. I've done my research. You see, there's no possible way that you can't win. On one side we have a gutter rat who's lived in the projects all her life, and that's all she knows. And then there's you. A bad motherfucker with the body of a goddess and as submissive as they come. I've just come by to groom you. Make sure you get that first place no matter what."

"I'm confused."

"Sit," Markiesha instructed her and pulled from her cigarette once more. After she blew her smoke, she mashed out the orange glow at the tip of it and smoothed her hands over the back of the couch until her arms were fully extended. "The last boyfriend you had was a pedal-pusher. You know what that is, don't you? A petty nigga who only slings nickel and dime sacks. A nothing. A nobody. But my son? I raised him to be the best. He's going to be a fucking king. You, Dena, are used to dealing with Diego's kind. Or should I say *Ramone's* kind? You know how to handle royalty. Shit, girl, you're a spitfire away from being a princess yourself... only you haven't found the right baller to put that tiara on your head yet."

"You don't know anything about me," Dena opposed skeptically.

"The shit I don't. Girl, I *was* you. And if you want half of one point five million dollars guaranteed, plus some after the wedding, then you'd stick with me to make sure that you never have to bow to another wannabe again."

"I don't want his money."

"You came here for love?" Markiesha laughed. She threw her head back and was tickled pink by the statement until she quickly composed herself and stared at Dena with a straight face. "Girl, love is an overrated emotion that will get you hurt and leave you lonely with the quickness. Now you can sit here and act like you're not reaching for the gold when I know for a fact that you've only had one job in the last two years, and that was being a dancer at a two-bit strip club. You say, with a clean face, that you only want my son for his heart when your rent is past due and they're close to repossessing your car? Hell, you ran away from home when you were fifteen and ended up getting pimped out by the time you turned seventeen, until your sugar daddy took you away and told you to work for your money. And that, my dear, is what landed you being butt naked at that nasty ass strip club in Columbus. You're lying to someone who knows your lifestyle all too well. Now if you want me to keep your secret agenda and help you stay relevant, you'll accept my help."

"Why are you willing to help me?"

"I don't need him with some hoodie who has nothing to offer him but the pot of piss she wallows in down there in the projects."

"If you think you know me so well then you would know that people change."

"You live by the sword, you die by the sword. Once you're in this life, almost *nothing* can change the cold blood in your veins."

"And what life is that?" Dena raised an eyebrow at Markiesha, even though she knew what she was getting at.

Markiesha reached into her handbag and pulled out a vile and a condom, and sat them both on the coffee table. "In this little tube is a mixture of eye drops and rum. Slip it into his drink and have your way with him. He won't remember a damn thing. Poke a hole in this condom before you take it out of the wrapper and make sure to tell him that you want to keep safe, just in case, he has a little memory of you two going at it. In nine months, say hello to your relevancy."

"And this is supposed to work?" she laughed.

"How in the hell do you think I'm able to walk around with an eleven-thousand-dollar handbag, sixteen-hundred-dollar shoes, and a suit that I had custom fitted? And by the way, I've only worn everything once before, and it was years ago. My closet, mini-mansion and car collection would slay your entire existence." Markiesha grabbed up her purse and strutted over to the door, but sharply turned to Dena on the balls of her heels. "You're pretty, by the way. Thicker lashes would really set off your makeup, though."

Dena watched as the wealthy woman left the apartment and took her eyes back to the contents on the table. She had a very heavy choice to make, but going back to the slums was not an option for her.

—

When Diego woke the next morning, he could've sworn someone had bashed him in the head with a hammer. His mouth was dry and opening his eyes was a tough task. He rolled over and ended up landing on Dena's arm. Quickly, he shifted in his bed as if her arm had been on fire and had singed his skin. "What the fuck?" he grumbled. He shoved her arm to get her awake and pulled back the covers to discover her naked body. His eyes had gone wide when looking at her mounds.

Never in his life had he moved so fast to get out of bed and snatch his phone up from the charger. He didn't care who he called as he sloppily shuffled around his home, just as long as he had gotten someone on the phone to verify that he wasn't dreaming. In the last two days that Dena had been with him, he stashed her in the third room which was one that Christina hadn't slept in.

On the third ring, Chandler answered for his friend. "What's good?" he hoarsely asked into his phone.

"Nigga," Diego panicked and dropped to his bottom in the furthest corner of his kitchen. His eyes almost fell out of his head while he tried to get his words together. "I think I fucked Dena last night."

"You think? What you mean, you think?"

"I woke up with this bitch naked in my bed, bro. My draws are fuckin' wet, my head is killing me and my dick is sore. It's either I fucked her hard as hell or she raped me. I don't even think niggas can get raped other than by another man, can they?"

"You're trippin' like a motherfucker right now."

"No, I'm not," he hissed. "I know what the fuck I feel like after I fucked a bitch."

"Then why is it an issue?"

"Why is it...?" Diego pulled himself off of the floor and jogged into his hall bathroom to whip out his snake and to drain it. Usually after a wild night with a female he didn't want, he'd have to pee for an extended period of time.

Chandler could hear when his fluid hit the water in the toilet, and it sounded like he had been going for longer than what he'd have to when waking up with morning wood. "Nigga, is it somethin' wrong with your prostate?" he asked him. "Why're you pissin' so damn long?"

"I fucked this bitch," Diego said sadly, even though he wasn't done relieving his bladder as of yet. "I swear, bro. I fucked this bitch. If Christina finds out—"

"She won't. I won't say shit. We just need a way to get her back to you. She's supposed to be graduating in two weeks, and you're supposed to have your dinner with both girls and your parents around that time. We can do some spectacular shit during that time to woo her over. We got this. Just keep what happened last night between us. I ain't Angel. Your secret is more than safe with me."

"Damn, bro," Diego whined, and banged his fist on the counter top. "I swear to fucking God I fucked this bitch. What the fuck was I thinking? I told myself that I wasn't gon' do that shit because I wasn't gon' cheat on Chrissy. Look what the fuck I just did."

"Stop trippin' out. What's done is done. Sweep it under the rug and keep it moving. We got this, Dutch. Besides, you were pretty fucked up last night. I got to bring your ride back to you before we go to Rachel's graduation."

Diego flushed the toilet and trapped his cellphone between his ear and his shoulder so that he could wash his hands. Just as he touched the knob, a thought came to him. "That's it," he announced. "I can get Rachel something nice before we go to her graduation, I can talk her into going to see Chrissy, and then I can start to win her back. I mean, she *has* to come to dinner. That's in the contract."

"Yea, but damn near killing your best friend wasn't."

Diego sucked his teeth. "Man, fuck you, Chandler."

"You almost shot me too, nigga! All 'cause you were mad!"

"He shouldn't have been a pussy, and you shouldn't have tried to save a pussy. On top of that, I said some ruthless shit to Chrissy. How the fuck am I going to win her back after that?"

"You're the Dutch," Chandler teased. "Ain't no such thing as not being able to do something. I gotta go, though. I'm going to bring you your ride in a little bit, so sober the fuck up so we can take this road trip. Oh, and don't forget that we got to stop and drop somethin' off on your daddy."

"Bet." Diego released the phone and caught it in his hand after he dried them both off and left the bathroom. When he entered his room, he took one look at Dena on the bed and it made his skin crawl.

He showered and slipped into a burgundy V-neck and a pair of pressed dark blue denim shorts, number 13 Jordan's that were white and burgundy, and grabbed his jewelry from his dresser so that he could leave without Dena even knowing.

# Chapter 14

Diego pulled Rachel outside of the restaurant where they gathered to have a celebratory dinner with her parents and friends after her graduation. Chandler's eyes were on her curves that had been stuffed inside of her calve-length pencil skirt and tight black button up blouse, and she turned around to push him into a nearby parking meter.

"You shouldn't be stacked, and I wouldn't look," Chandler complained. He caught his balance and fondly wrapped an arm around her neck as she rolled her eyes at him.

"Look, Dutch, I will talk to her," Rachel said. Then she punched him in the shoulder.

"What the fuck was that for?" he screamed at her.

"Because you fucked up! You paid for an abortion and made the girl shut up about it!"

"I did it to save my relationship before it even started!"

"Did you even stop to think of what that baby could've meant to that girl? Huh? Did you stop to think of if she even wanted it? This is why Christina is mad at you. Girls take abortions seriously, motherfucker, and you just had to do it. And on top of that, you kept it away from her. Women don't like to have secrets between our partners and us in relationships."

"I know that now but I need her. I said some real reckless shit the other day, and—"

"Oh my Gooood! You just can't stop, can you? How long have I known you, Dutch?"

"Since I tried to fuck with you, freshman year."

"Since then. And we were fourteen. We're twenty-two. That's a long time. With that being said, I know that you've never been desperate a day in your damn life, so I'm going to help you out, but I can't make any promises."

"Your daddy makes promises," he mumbled.

"I'm not him," she hissed. "I'm not a damn hitman under contract with your father. I may be Haitian, but I'm not damn Super Woman."

"Wait," Chandler intervened and leaned away from Rachel. "That nigga in there with the long ass hair is your daddy right?"

"Right."

"He's a Haitian?"

"Chandler, where the fuck have you been?"

"Chasing after you, but I didn't know your old man was a hitman."

"How did you think he made his money? He can't work for anyone with all that hair on his head or the permanent grimace on his face."

"Damn. I learn something new every day. In finding that out, I should let you know that things would've never worked between us, Rachel. I mean, you're sexy as fuck, and you may be a lesbian, but I don't want to be killed by your daddy."

"Shut up," she gritted. "Dutch, add on to your lady problems with the fact that you still have business to do with my dad over your territory issues. Looks like you have to bust knuckles to finally call yourself a man. But I'll give it to you that you're trying. At least you reached out for help. I'll go by and talk to her in a couple of days."

"*Days*?" he shrieked.

"I need some alone time with my girlfriend before she goes home to Ohio for good! I don't know what y'all thought might've changed for me, but I still come before any of you niggas." Rachel rolled her eyes and shoved Chandler one last time before going back into the restaurant to rejoin her family so that they all could part for a few months.

"What are you thinking?" Chandler asked him.

"I'm thinking that I need to make the rest of these few days with Dena fly the fuck by to get her out of my face, and finally pray to God that Christina sees the light."

"And your job?"

He removed his Aviator shades and rubbed the tip of the arm of them against his bottom lip while thinking. "I work best under pressure. This shit is all a breeze somehow, and I'm making a hell of a lot more money than I was before. I produce more product, deliver more, and still give my old man his sixty percent. On top of that, he gave me a bonus the day that Angel snitched me out. All that shit in that duffle bag was money."

"Nightlife?"

"Nigga, *work life*. I'm gonna have a tuition to pay. I need to stack and save and get ready to help Chrissy take care of her mama. I might be scared, but I'm still confident as shit that she's gonna break down."

"You know I got you. Let me know what you need from me." Chandler gave him a fist pound and threw his shades on so that he could tag along and help his friend take care of business for the rest of the night. He just needed to help his friend get through Thursday, Friday and Saturday, and then they'd be home free to win Christina over.

―――

Christina, tired of being sent roses and cards, sorry pleas and all, sat at the dinner table at an expensive restaurant before anyone else had arrived. She seethed. Her leg wouldn't stop dancing underneath the table because of the conversation she had with Rachel the night before.

She was busy scrubbing the kitchen floor with a bandanna tied over her hair and rubber gloves clad on her hands that made her skin moist. She received a knock on the backdoor and looked up at it as if she could see through the small square blinds and out of the window, though she had been on her hands and knees. She raised from the strong smell of lavender Fabuloso on the linoleum and opened the door to find Rachel there, dressed in a pair of short cut off denim shorts, white muscle shirt and a pair of Chuck Taylor's.

Rachel slowly stepped inside and closed the door behind her, hopped over the glistening parts of the floor and balanced herself on the carpet in the living room. She then removed her oversized shades and placed her hand on her hip. "And this is how you're going to spend your day before you go in to meet the parents?" she asked smartly, and fit her shades on top of her head over her long spiral curls. Rachel rolled her eyes and ventured over to the couch and plopped down onto it.

"Why are you here?" Christina asked defensively while pulling off her gloves. "If you're here to convince me to go to that dinner tomorrow, you can save it because I'm not going. Your friend—"

"Was a man who thought that he was doing something right, even though it was stupid as fuck. I know. And after that he said some shit to you that he didn't mean because you hurt him, so he lashed out at you and has been wishing that he could take it back ever since. But what you need to do is ask yourself why you even care?"

"I *don't*," Christina retorted.

"Bullshit, lies and pies. Christina, you love that man, and you don't want to."

"You don't know shit about me." Christina folded her arms and leaned her back against the wall near the couch to stare down at Rachel. If only she knew what a dangerous woman Rachel was, she would've just kept quiet and listened.

"I know that all of that is just faux armor." She reached out and mocked rubbing her hands all over Christina's body. "I know that you've been hurt so you put up a wall to keep others out because you don't like disappointment and neglect. How do I know? Because you never took the time to get to know me in order to find out that I was the same way. Shit, I just wanted head and threw the bitches away after that, because I didn't want to give them the opportunity to hurt me. I didn't want any downfalls, so I used them and that was it. I was living for me and me only and put on a bad bitch attitude just to keep them all away. But here is where you fucked up. If you knew what type of person Dutch was before you, then you'd know that he made changes specifically *for* you."

"I saw that," she said smartly.

"Then you shouldn't have left. The reason you ran is because you just couldn't face it and you panicked at the fact that he gave you a sign of weakness. You're thinking that there are more lies and secrets. You're thinking that he played with you for his own thrill. But he didn't, Chris. Dutch plays way worse games than lying and keeping secrets. He's a brutally honest man who wouldn't give a fuck about what you or anybody else felt. So you need to think about the sacrifice he made to balance the first job that he ever had while trying to give you time. Dutch never gives a bitch anything, but he gave you his most prized possession. Chris, he gave you himself. Now

I expect you to be at dinner tomorrow night, because if not, then you're something that I thought you weren't. You're not strong enough. Believe me, when I say that you even fooled me into thinking that you were a brave girl with a good heart, who had her head sitting straight on her shoulders. You're going to leave me as a liar… and trust me… I've *never* been that. Especially not to someone I consider an estranged brother." Rachel raised from the couch and sashayed out of the front door as if she made valuable points. It left Christina with flaring nostrils.

How dare she show up and tell her about herself? Now she sat at the table, dodging a kiss when Diego leaned down to peck her cheek. She turned her head away when he was a gentleman and pulled out Dena's chair for her. She hadn't known about their only dinner together and how Diego really hadn't kept up conversation with the young woman, or him avoiding her by having Chandler to constantly come over to keep him company, by distracting him with social media. If she kept up with her Tumblr page, then she should've noticed how something was off with how much he'd been snapping single photos of himself, broadcasting his swag and the things he'd been eating, smoking and doing. None of which included Dena.

"How are we tonight?" Ramone asked as he approached the table. He quickly pecked the girls' cheeks and patted his son on the back before taking his seat. "Christina, are you excited about graduation?" Ramon unclasped his cufflinks while looking over the young girl's black romper he sent to her a few days prior. He was actually surprised that it fit. He figured then that he hadn't lost his touch when it came to eyeing women and gifting them garments.

"Thrilled," she dryly replied.

"How's Ms. Jackson? She being released soon?"

"She's coming home in two days."

"Good. I thought she'd make a full recovery."

"Please, don't start speaking to them before I arrive," Markiesha sang. She basically floated over to the table and waited for Ramone to pull her chair out for her. When he took a sip of his water from his water glass, her skin heated. She reached for the back of her chair, but he'd pulled it out by the leg while keeping his eyes on the table. "Thank you," Markiesha said with a grin and sat so that they could get to interviewing the girls. She swiped her short ringlet curls behind her ears and shared a quick glance with Dena. "So, Christina, is it? I'm not familiar with you. Can you tell me a little bit about yourself?"

"There's not much to tell," she replied with a lazy tongue. "College student, take care of my mama, have a career plan, and I'm a homebody."

"You don't seem like you're interested in being here. If you want, you can leave."

Ramone pinched Markiesha's bare thigh underneath the table, and she slapped his hand away. "Dena, what about you?"

"I'm sure that my life isn't as *extravagant* as Christina's." She scooted a little closer to Diego and clasped her hands over the tabletop. "I was an aspiring model for a little bit. I have an impressive portfolio, but I don't care much for the glitz and the flashing cameras. I want to settle down and have a family, and just be a supportive housewife."

"Sounds charming." Markiesha smiled at her, then looked over at her son. "Diego, doesn't that sound *charming* to you?"

"Yea, very charming," he hurriedly replied. "Daddy, are you okay after everything that's happened?"

"Hmm?" He swallowed the last little bit of his water and nodded. "Yea, I'm okay. I'm good. I just learned to keep potential predators at arms-length."

"Uh, we won't be talking about business at this table," Markiesha announced. "We have two possible brides for our son, Ramone."

"Speak like you have sense, Kiesh. We don't want our son getting up and walking away from this table, do we?"

"Y'all, come on now," Diego interjected. "Get your questions out of the way."

"Yes, please do," Dena backed him eagerly. "I'm looking forward to getting to know the family."

"Family," Christina mumbled.

Markiesha scowled at the young woman who sat in front of her. "What was that?"

"Ask your questions so that I can leave, please."

"You know, Christina, this is a once in a lifetime chance," Dena said. "If you didn't want to participate then you shouldn't have entered."

"I *didn't*," she snapped.

"Nuh uh! We won't have that ghetto mess in this restaurant," Markiesha proclaimed.

"Then why did *you* even show up?"

"You little hood rat ass—"

"Markiesha, you better watch your mouth," Diego warned her.

Dena grabbed his arm and stated, "But you won't be taking up for her."

"And who the fuck are you to tell me who I can and can't defend?"

"Son," Ramone gritted. "A king holds his composure and speaks with finality."

"You *won't* tell me who I can and can't defend. Fall back."

"I don't need you to help me," Christina spoke. "You should be trying to help yourself."

"And you're sure she's top two material?" Markiesha laughed. "Please. Choose the next best thing. But of course, we don't see a broad picking her nose and scratching her ass in public."

"You know what? You don't even have the right to look me in the fucking face, you materialistic bitch."

"Excuse me?"

Christina raised out of her seat, and so did Dena. "You need to try and be a mother before you sit at a panel to try and decide your son's fate."

"You're rude as hell, and I'm glad that Diego doesn't see anything in you," Dena scoffed.

"Oh, he doesn't?" Her head whirled around to the stacked and glamorous young woman with fire in her eyes. "Then you tell me what his middle name is, what his favorite color and food is. But you can't, can you? But I bet you know what his dick tastes like and what his net worth is."

"Christina, please calm down," Ramone begged her. "Sit. We'll start all over."

"She's not fit to eat with us," Markiesha remarked.

Christina banged her hand on the table. "Fuck this! No, I'm not fit to sit at this table and be criticized by a woman who cherishes a hundred-dollar bill over the wellbeing of her own son, and some plastic ass bitch, who I'm more than sure was a high paid hooker before she got into this circus act. I don't need the money, the drama, the bullshit, and I definitely don't need any of you. Bitch, you can have him because Ramone's money is what's more important to all of you. But at the end of the day, the both of you bitches will never have enough backbone to do what the fuck I do in a day, and that's why you hoes are bottom-feeders. You're not fit to eat with *me*. Facts fucking straightened."

"Babe!" Diego reached out for her just as she turned away and marched out of the restaurant.

Ramone raised a brow at his son and rolled his eyes to the door to signal for him to go after her. Unfortunately, he was too late. By the time he shuffled through a party crowd at the front door, Christina was getting on a bus across the street. He unbuttoned his skinny black vest and fished his valet ticket from his pocket. She had a 10-minute head start with how long the valet took to get his car but seeing as how he'd passed the bus en route to the projects, he parked at the corner store and got out of his SUV to lean against the hood for when she stepped off the bus. There wasn't a way that she could slip past him this time.

Not long after he loosened his necktie, the bus crept close to the designated stop and Christina stepped off with a frown on her face. He tilted his head at her and stuffed his hands inside the pockets of his slacks.

"What?" she asked with attitude in her voice. "You come out here to scold me because you got into trouble with your bitch and your *mommy*?"

"Chill on that 'mommy' shit, alright? You know how I feel about her."

Christina rolled her eyes and stepped out of a pair of black imitation leather heels that were killing her feet. "You know what's funny?" she quietly laughed as she sloppily strolled over to him on bare feet. "I actually wore heels tonight, because absentmindedly, I was trying to compete with the next bitch and grab your attention. I wanted you to be mad at me for being so damn cute today and realize how you've fucked up. I didn't need to because as soon as I saw you from my peripheral, you looked so pitiful. I have to commend you on the change you've made from being the snot-ball you were when we met to this charming prince that was underneath your skin all along. But... this is not what *I* want."

Diego frowned, and his heart could've landed on his own feet.

"I had fun, I felt loved and cherished, but I also felt the sting of hurt."

"Chris—"

"I don't ever want to feel that again," she cut him off with her stern statement. "I also forgot to check in on my mama. I got caught up and missed a day of my lecture. Never again will I do that in the future. Yes, I accept your apology, and I forgive you for what you did. Even for talking to me like you were stupid because I provoked you with my attitude. I too apologize for what I said and how I acted."

"Chrissy, listen to me—"

"Maybe one of these days we'll actually be able to be real friends. Maybe one day we'll even be lovers again. Today, tomorrow, sometime within the following year won't be that day."

"Chris, don't do this to me."

"I'm doing it to me too, Diego." The tail end of her sentence faded out while her eyes clouded. "This is going to hurt me way worse than what I thought you did to me, but it's something that needs to be done."

"I chose you! You knew I did!"

"Yea... but I *don't* choose you." Sadly, she turned away to keep her falling tears away from view and took her walk across the street to her apartment unit.

"Chrissy!" he called after her. "Christina, get back here! Baby, I'm in love with you!"

Christina stopped breathing altogether after hearing the magic words that any woman wanted to hear. She slowly turned around to see him standing there with his arms spread out and a look of desperation on his face. "What did you say?"

He jogged across the street and grabbed her face within his palms to stare into her glassed eyes. "I said that I love you, Christina. You're killing a nigga out here."

"Diego—"

"You want me to forfeit the money?"

"I wouldn't ask you to throw away Ramone's legacy."

"No, fuck it. I'll give up the trust fund, the trappin', all of it just so I can have you. You're worth more to me than that. Why can't you see that?"

"I can't—"

"Goddamn! Let go of all of that other bullshit and see me!" He flailed his arms and stepped away from her. "What is it that you want me to do? Huh? You want me to open my skin and bleed out for you? Because if that's what you want then all you're going to see is images of you! You're in my fuckin' veins, girl! Tell me you don't love me! Say that shit and I'll go! I'll leave you the fuck alone, and I will never bother you again. I'll take that trust fund money and move out of the fuckin' country. So say it. Say that shit so I can back the fuck off."

Christina bit her lip to keep her tears at bay, but it wasn't working. They splashed her cheeks while she battled with closing herself up or staying open and honest with him.

"Tell me, Christina! Say it!"

"I love you!" she shouted back. "Don't fucking hurt me! I don't want the drama! I don't want the bullshit business either!"

"I'll keep it all away from you, baby." He softened his tone then and latched on to her hips to bring her closer to him. "I swear. I won't do anything to make you uncomfortable. So you'll stay?"

"I'm scared," she cried. "I don't want you to turn on me. I don't want you to make me empty promises or run off and leave me because I can't have kids."

Diego pulled away and grimaced at her. "So this is what all of this about?" he asked. "You think I'm gonna turn out to be like your old man? Christina, I didn't plan on leaving you when I knew that you were the one. And dammit, if we can't have kids then we can adopt. I'm nothing like him. I will love you until you force me not to with your attitude."

"And what about my mama? I can't leave her."

"We won't leave her. You can teach me your routine if you have to so that I can help."

"It'll be too much when you work a lot as is—"

He lifted her chin with the crook of his pointer finger to deliver his message. "Stop making excuses. Any and everything is possible. Just like you make your schedule flexible, I can do the same. Even if all we do is say hello when we hit the bed, then I'm fine with that knowing that the house and your mama is okay at the end of the day. As long as I have you, I'm willing to make it work."

"I'm going to trust you this one time," she sniffled. "I promise you that if you fuck me over, you can forget about me and my mama."

"So that's a yes?" he grinned. "We're going to do this?"

"Yes," she whined as she stomped her foot on the ground.

"My Chrissy doesn't fuckin' whine." He laid a promising kiss on her lips to seal their agreement. If Diego had it his way, he would've turned cartwheels in the street, but he had to keep his composure only for the moment.

# Epilogue

***One Month Later...***

Markiesha sat on the side of her bed while waiting for Dena to finally emerge from her master bathroom. For the entire day, she had the girl chugging down water to take multiple pregnancy tests. She had to be sure before she carted the girl into an OBGYN to have a specialist look at her and take sonograms of her new meal ticket. Since the announcement at the block party, a few weeks prior, that Diego was choosing Christina, Dena had to puke behind the platform they stood on but Markiesha kept her composure. She didn't care if Dena was really in it for love, she wasn't going to let her fuck up the chance at snagging her funds to start a new business venture so that she'd have her continuous cash flow.

Dena held her stomach while shutting off the light in the bathroom and handed Markiesha the little white stick she peed on. Markiesha took one look at the window and smiled.

"Well that makes the tenth test you've taken that read positive," she nonchalantly said. "Next trip is to the clinic to get proof. In two months, we'll have a wedding to stop, and you'll be rolling in cash. But if you don't want to look like a sneaky little *whore*, you'd cut me in and keep your mouth closed."

"What?" Dena gasped.

Markiesha escorted her down the stairs, grabbed Dena's purse off the coatrack near the door and offered up a warm smile for her. "Never sign a verbal contract with the devil before reading the small print, dear. You have a nice evening and leave the rest up to me."

"You said nothing about—"

Markiesha opened the front door and pressed her back against it to wait for the troubled soul to leave. "This is a battle for the crown. Either you want it, or you don't. You can have it. I just want the *money*. Ciao."

Dena frowned at the woman who happily waved her goodbye when everything she had gotten herself into hit her at once. She was stuck, and there was no way out of it. Even if she decided to get rid of the baby, there was no telling what Markiesha could've opened up and said about her and the reasons why she'd get rid of it. Dena was more than sick. She hated herself for stepping into a new league of gold digging.

***To be continued…***

# Acknowledgements

Seeing as how I'm never really good at these things— and I really don't like to copy and paste— let's start off by acknowledging the Man upstairs for the talents he's blessed me with. Without it, I'd be absolutely nothing with no meaning or course in life. Secondly, let's shine that good old spotlight on my mother who is the rock and the matriarch of a very strong and intelligent family. I love you, mommy! (Please don't call and yell at me when you're done reading this piece. Please, and thank you. *KISSES*!)

At the current time, I feel as if I'm living a mere dream to be able to disappear and come back to my readers, only to be accepted as though I never left. You guys are amazing. Had it not been for you, I don't believe I'd still be penning anything. All I ask of you is that you don't let me fall. Continue to let me float throughout this fantasy of mine as if I'm not really living it. Can we do that?

To my Angel— my right hand and the only woman outside of my family that I absolutely cannot live without— thank you for always being there, whether I needed you or not. I don't mean to make us sound old, being that we're only 26 and 27 years, but you started reading my work at age 14 and hadn't stopped yet. I truly appreciate your random outbursts and sarcasm, the way you lose your temper and refuse to speak to me unless I give you at least close to a happy ending. I love you, short stacks.

Shaniqua Desha, you're so awesome and talented, and I don't even think you realize how truly gifted you are. Hopefully you will and you'll let those flaming wings of yours fly free and never let them go dim. Thank you for test reading for me. I can always count on your honest opinion and your support. Maybe one day we'll sit back and laugh at the shadiness in the business, and recall all of the times that the both of us wanted to throw in the towel, but end up laughing at one another hysterically because we're still standing and happy with how we ended our careers. Keep your head up, little one. Dark times don't always last, and pain is only temporary.

[Author] Chrissy J, you know where we stand. You're my author soulmate, and if you were a lesbian I swear I would've married you two years ago. *JUST KIDDING*! Seriously though, I love you in some unexplainable way— that's not sexual, or lustful— and no one else understands it but us. You've been my Ace Boon Coon since, literally, the first day that I was introduced into this business. Your place is written in stone. You're the realest that I know and I'm grateful that you've been here for the wild ride we've shared. Thank you for everything.

*THE SQUAD*! [Authors] Larissa, Lola Bandz and Jasmine Devonish, y'all are mad ill, for real. Did y'all know? Seriously, they say keep your circle small for a reason, and I truly know what that means. Only you remain from the original some odd people that I started with. I've seen them come and go in this business, but never have either of you pushed a blade into my ribs for any reason, or turned your backs on me. The closeness that we have is irreplaceable, so let no man or woman put asunder. Raise your glasses to success because that's all we've seen thus far. We may stray, but we don't stray far and never forget one another; whether we feel we're at the bottom, or whether we're at the top taking in the scenery. You're my sisters and I would say I love y'all, but that's that gay ish. *HUGS*!

Leo [Sullivan], you may think that all of your wise words went into one ear and out of the other, but they didn't. You have no idea how— every time I felt like doing something foolish— I could hear you as clear as crystal in my ear, saying, "You're gonna be standing when their light dies out. You're a talented motherf****er and you're wastin' it with this bulls***." Thank you. I gave you a hard time when all I had to do was grab my imaginary testes and crank you out another banger. But noooo, I just had to fall into the childishness and swell my chest with that "entitled" crap. So now is the time when I apologize for the cruel words and the wasted time that can't be returned or relived. I apologize for being so spoiled rotten, and for throwing tantrums when I should've trusted you. Still, your lessons and your conversations stick with me. Everything positive that you've ever said is finally being lived. It shouldn't have taken this long, but it doesn't go in vain, sir. Lastly, thank you for taking a chance on me once more. I mean, it's no secret that if I couldn't bang a series, you probably would've cussed me out and gave me a solid "Hell naw!" but we're not going to bring that up. Love you lots for what you've done, what you've said, what you've proved, and most of all for what you've taught... *old man*. Look on the bright side though. I get to bother you again! Yay, us!

Porscha Sterling— the woman with the S on her chest. You know what I found odd? How you see and hear everything. Who knew that you knew anything about me? When do you sleep? What planet are you from? I won't tell anyone. I promise. On a serious note, I thank you for being brave enough to take on the project that is Sunny Giovanni and for being involved with this title. It's not many publishers who don't show favoritism and who will equally promote their authors and their brand, and you're sincerely one of them. I have one in the flesh and I'm proud to say that. With you in my corner now, I feel like the stratosphere is the limit and I can actually see me going there (possibly to your home planet so that you can show me where there are more of you). There's something about you that made me want to write, and write some more. And when this specific project was done, I couldn't stop. I needed to write a little more. Now I see how Royalty Publishing House spits out books the way they do with the positive energy and the fact that no one person is above the other. This business needs more publishers like you. I'm blessed to have you, though. *IN YOUR FACE, LIT WORLD! SHE'S MINE!*

To the awesome, amazing, astounding, talented, energetic, studious, versatile and gorgeous women of RHP, it's an extreme honor to be working with you all! Amongst other things, it's a pleasure to read the dopest books I've read in a while, from the dopest women I've ever come in contact with. You authors are genuine and sincere, and some of your posts have me wanting to pinch myself to see if I'm awake or if I'm imagining things. With so much positivity in one place… it's almost indescribable. Thank you all for the kindness and the support, and thank you for showing me that people aren't fake when they smile in your face. I wish I could share you… but I don't think I'll be doing that. Thank you guys!

Last, but not least, my Trojan. You know what it is and you know how I feel. Thank you for the sacrifice you made years ago. Without it, none of this would be possible. I wish you would think of not claiming me. I don't have any restraining orders, but that'll be the day that I get one. Try it if you'd like. I love you, LeQuintis— my best friend, the father of my children, and the architect of my career.

Looking for a publishing home?

Royalty Publishing House, Where the Royals reside, is accepting submissions for writers in the urban fiction genre. If you're interested, submit the first 3-4 chapters with your synopsis to submissions@royaltypublishinghouse.com.

Check out our website for more information: www.royaltypublishinghouse.com.

Be sure to LIKE our Royalty Publishing House page on Facebook

CPSIA information can be obtained
at www.ICGtesting.com
Printed in the USA
LVOW07s1551170517
534871LV00010B/799/P